The GOLDEN EAGLE Mystery

BY ELLERY QUEEN, JR.

Illustrated by Charles Beck

SCHOLASTIC BOOK SERVICES

Published by Scholastic Book Services, a division of Scholastic Magazines, Inc., New York, N.Y.

Single copy price 50¢ (includes postage).
Quantity prices available on request.

 This Scholastic Book Services edition is published by arrangement with J. B. Lippincott Company.

3rd printing........................October 1962

Printed in the U.S.A.

CONTENTS

Other Books by Ellery Queen, Jr.

The Green Turtle Mystery*
The White Elephant Mystery
The Yellow Cat Mystery
The Black Dog Mystery
The Red Chipmunk Mystery
The Blue Herring Mystery
The Brown Fox Mystery

*A TAB Book selection for Teen Age Book Club

1. Alberto

THE NEW boy closed the front door behind him and looked up and down the unfamiliar street. He was eager to explore the village. He was eager to meet the people who lived there. He hoped, anxiously, that some one would tell him something about Aunt Patty Tubbs, at whose house he was to stay that summer. One thing was sure: he must not ask Aunt Patty herself.

Over and over he repeated to himself, as he stood there on the front steps of the little house, the instructions he had been given before he left home:

"Go and find out what the trouble is at Aunt Patty's house. There's trouble of some sort. She may even be in great danger. But, if you ask her, she will probably say that there's nothing wrong at all. Just go there and keep your ears open. You will like that town, anyway. You will have fun there. It's a nice place to spend the summer. Just do what Aunt Patty asks you to do, and don't bother her with questions. Listen to what her neighbors say, there in Stony Harbor, and find out for yourself what is worrying her. No one need ever guess that a boy like you is a real detective."

So there he was, in Stony Harbor, and wondering excitedly what he would find. The village looked very peaceful. Aunt Patty's house was a tiny little cottage, on a street of little white houses. The dazzling blue sky overhead made them seem even whiter than white. Each one had a tiny front yard, not much bigger than a handkerchief, separated from the street by a fence of wooden pickets, also painted white. Each little yard was full of bright-colored flowers. On the porch of the house across the street a very comfortable-looking yellow cat with white rings around its tail was dozing in the sun.

The new boy turned around and spoke to the shaggy little black Scotty terrier which had followed him out of the house and which was now pulling at his leash. The dog's hair was so long and tangled that you could hardly see his sharp eyes, like bright black shoe-buttons.

"Now, listen," said the boy. "No chasing cats, Champ, do you hear?"

Champ wagged his short little tail.

"You're telling *me?*" he asked pleasantly. "Whose nose got scratched last time, yours or mine?"

"All right, let's go, then," said the boy. "But remember!"

They set off down the street, keeping their eyes open. Looking to the left, between two houses, the boy saw a gleam of blue water, bluer than the sky, and the clustered masts of small sailboats at a pier, only a little way off.

"Oh, boy!" he exclaimed, softly, "maybe we can go sailing!"

They walked on a few steps, passed another house, and this time the boy looked toward the right. Again he saw the gleam of bright blue water, framed between the houses, and it was so close that he could easily have thrown a stone into it.

"Oh, boy!" he said again, louder this time. "Water everywhere! And, look, Champ, there's a diving platform out there! This is going to be *good!*"

Champ sniffed, through his long black whiskers. He didn't think much of swimming. His legs were too short.

They walked on. A little ahead of them, the street divided in two and enclosed a little green park, not much more than thirty feet square. Tall elm trees grew around it, and on the grass stood two old cannon, on wheels, their noses pointing out over the water to right and left. Between them was a low stone monument; and in front of the monument stood a boy. He had his back to them; and he was so interested in what he was doing that he didn't hear them coming.

The new boy and his little black dog came a little closer, and then stopped. The other boy was talking to someone.

"Alberto!" he said sharply. "That's not the way to do it!"

The boy who had just come to town wondered who Alberto could be. He couldn't see anyone else beside the boy who was talking.

Alberto is standing on the other side of the monument, of course, where he can't be seen, the new boy thought to himself. He must be pretty small.

"Alberto!" said the other boy, once more. "Up! Up on your hind legs!"

Oh, thought the new boy, it's a dog! No wonder I couldn't see him!

"There, that's better!" said the other boy, snapping his fingers. "That's right, walk! *Now* you've got it! Down, now, Alberto, and do the headstand! Up on your hands, now! Up! That's right! Now take a step. That's right, Alberto, you're doing fine! Walk toward me! That's it, that's the way! Good for you!"

The new boy was burning with curiosity. A dog walking on its front paws! Why, you would never see a dog like that, outside of a circus! He certainly must see that dog, or he would burst. He took a fresh grip on Champ's leash, just in case the other dog might not be friendly, and stepped up on the grass.

The other boy heard him now, and turned around.

He was about the same age as the first boy, but he was taller and thinner. He was so tall and thin that he looked willowy. But he wasn't sick-looking. His face was tanned as brown as a berry, and he stepped forward as though he was moving on springs.

"Hello!" he said quickly, even before the new boy could speak. "I never heard you coming! Gee, you don't make any more noise than an Indian! Say, you're new around here, aren't you? What's *your* name? Is that your dog? Scotty, isn't he? Say, he's a dandy! What's *his* name? Gee, I wish I had a dog like that! You don't live here in Stony Harbor, do you? Been here long? Where you come from? Like it here? What you say your name was? *My* name's Billy Reckless. Wanta fight?"

He laughed when he said it, and he had been grinning all the time, while the words came tumbling out of him, so the new boy laughed, too.

"No," he said. "But, gee, I'd like to see your dog!"

The thin boy laughed again. "You mean Alberto?" he asked. 'Sure, I'll show him to you, sometime. What's your name?"

"Djuna," said the new boy.

"Joona? How do you spell it?" asked the thin boy.

The new boy told him.

"Gee, that's a funny one!" said the thin boy. "First time I ever heard *that* name! Where do you live?"

"Well, I live at Miss Annie Ellery's house, in a place called Edenboro," said Djuna, "but it's an awful long way from here. I just got here today. I'm going to stay here at Mrs. Tubbs' house. All summer, I guess. Say, let's see your dog!"

Billy Reckless paid no attention to the question. "Mrs. Tubbs?" he repeated. "You mean Aunt Patty. How did you happen to come here?"

"Oh, is she your aunt?" asked Djuna.

"Oh, no," said Billy. "Everybody calls her Aunt Patty, that's all. Didn't you know that?"

"How could I?" retorted Djuna. "I just got here today, I tell you. Miss Ellery wrote to her, and asked her if I could stay with her, because Miss Ellery used to know her, so she said yes. Say, listen, call Alberto, won't you?"

"Me, call Alberto?" said the thin boy, looking at Djuna thoughtfully. "I don't know whether I'd better call him, or not. How do I know your dog wouldn't chew him up?"

Djuna laughed. "Oh, don't you worry about that," he said. "Champ never starts a fight. He's very friendly."

Champ wagged his tail, as he always did whenever he heard his name spoken.

"And besides," added Djuna, seeing that the thin boy still hesitated, "I've got him on the leash. He *can't* get away. Go on, call Alberto!"

Billy Reckless' thin brown face lit up with a smile. "Say!" he exclaimed. "You really *like* dogs, don't you? All right, then, I'll tell you about Alberto. I'll tell you how I happened to get him. Come on, let's sit down over here in the shade, and I'll tell you the whole thing, cross my heart."

He led the way, and sat down on the low stone coping that surrounded the little square. Djuna followed, but he was puzzled.

"I don't mind waiting," he said, "but, look here, supposing your dog runs off, while we're talking? And I haven't even seen him yet!"

Billy laughed. "Don't worry," he said. "He won't run off. He can't."

Djuna sat down, unconvinced, and still keeping his eyes on the low stone monument. Alberto remained out of sight behind it, not making a sound.

"Why can't he run away?" Djuna demanded. "Is he tied there? No, I don't see how he could be, not while he was doing all those tricks. Hurry up, won't you?"

Billy smiled in a tantalizing sort of way.

"There's no hurry," he said. "As soon as I tell you where I got him, you'll see why."

"Go ahead, then!" begged Djuna.

"Well," said Billy, "the first time I thought of Alberto was about a year ago."

"Thought of him?" exclaimed Djuna, round-eyed.

"Sure. I didn't have any dog, then. And I wanted a good dog. I had a name all picked out for him. I was going to call him Alberto. I think that's a dandy name for a dog, don't you?"

"Well, yes, I guess so," said Djuna, slowly. "I don't believe I ever heard of a dog named Alberto before."

"Of course not!" said the thin boy proudly. "I made it up. Well, so then I had a name for my dog, all ready for him, but no dog. I was in a sort of a fix for an awful long time, that way. Had the name all ready, and no dog to give it to."

"Couldn't you get one?" asked Djuna, sympathetically.

"Didn't have any money," said the thin boy, promptly.

"Oh!" said Djuna. "What did you do?"

"Well, of course I began saving up money, whenever I could earn some—you know, running errands and things like that—but it took an awful long time. So then one day, all of a sudden, I got an idea. I thought I might just as well get some use of the name, while I was waiting for my dog. So I began practicing with it."

"Practicing?" exclaimed Djuna. "What do you mean?"

"When I was walking along the street, of course," Billy explained, grinning. "I'd whistle, and then I'd yell, 'Alberto, come here! Alberto! Alberto!' I had to get used to calling him the right way, didn't I?"

Djuna looked quickly over at the monument but no dog came out from behind it. Then he looked back at Billy.

"Go on," he said. "I'm listening."

"Well," said the thin boy, "the first thing I knew, when I was practicing calling Alberto one day, Old Man Truelove happened to come along, and he heard me. 'What's the matter?' he said. 'Lost your dog?' And I said, 'No, sir, I haven't lost him.' Which was true, of course, because I hadn't ever had him."

"Who's Mister Truelove?" asked Djuna.

"Oh, he runs the store down at his pier," said Billy, carelessly. "Phinny Truelove. Everybody knows him."

"Well, go on," said Djuna.

"Well, that's what gave me the idea," Billy continued. "All of a sudden I thought to myself, 'Why shouldn't I–' "

Djuna, who had been listening with eager attention, stopped Billy right in the middle of the sentence, by a whoop of admiration.

"Yippee!" he shouted. "Gee, that was a swell idea, Billy! Golly. I'll bet you have an awful lot of fun with him! For Pete's sake, that's the smartest thing I ever heard of!"

"Do you really think so?" asked the thin boy, anxiously. "Honest?"

"I certainly do!" said Djuna. "Why, you could do almost anything with a dog like that!"

Billy Reckless held out his hand. "Shake!" he said solemnly. "I could tell right away, as soon as I saw you, that we could be partners."

"I'd like to be," said Djuna, and he shook hands hard. "Say, is Alberto a collie? I always thought I'd like a collie, if I could have another dog besides Champ."

"He can be a collie, if you want," said Billy. "He changes, you know. Right now, I've had him be a fox terrier, because it's easier to teach fox terriers to do tricks. That's what I was doing when you came along. Want to see him?"

"Sure!" said Djuna.

So Billy Reckless proudly whistled to his imaginary dog, and the imaginary Alberto came bounding out from behind the stone monument, and the two boys put him through all his imaginary tricks. Alberto walked on his hind legs. Alberto walked on his front paws. Alberto answered questions. If he gave one bark, the answer was "Yes," if he gave two, the answer was "No," Billy explained.

But if anyone had happened to come along just then, they would not have seen two boys and two dogs—they would have seen only one dog, the small black Scotty named Champ, who sat patiently looking on while the two boys talked to Alberto, the dog that Billy Reckless had made up.

* * *

"Were you going anywhere special?" asked Billy Reckless, after they had put Alberto through all the tricks they could think of.

"Yes," said Djuna. "I was going to the grocery store to get some cans of dog food and some dog biscuits for Champ."

"I suppose I ought to get some for Alberto," said Billy, thoughtfully. "Shall I get you something to eat, Alberto?"

He listened for a moment and then grinned.

"He barked twice," he said to Djuna. "That means no."

"All right for *him*," said Djuna. "If he doesn't want any,

that's not *our* fault. Say, where is the grocery store, anyway, Billy?"

"We might as well go to Phinny Truelove's, I suppose," said Billy. "It's right around this corner, down at his dock. Come on, I'll show you."

Followed by Champ, at the end of his leash, the two boys set off. Alberto trotted ahead, easily invisible.

Mr. Phineas Truelove's store came into sight as soon as they turned the corner. It was right at the edge of the water, and beyond it were many boats anchored in the harbor.

To get to the store, they first passed through a vacant lot, where the ground was so stony and gravelly that not even weeds grew there. But it made a very good place for the fishermen to put things they were not using. On the edge of this lot, nearest the water, two or three old rowboats had been pulled up. In another part of the lot was a pile of wooden crates, one on top of another, and Djuna thought they looked like the crates that oranges are packed in.

"What are all those boxes for?" asked Djuna, pointing at them.

"Boxes?" asked Billy. "Oh, those aren't boxes, they're lobster pots!"

"You mean that's the way you catch lobsters?" asked Djuna. "I never saw any before."

"Sure," said Billy. "You see this little net with a hole in the middle, that's fastened to the end of each box? Well, the lobster goes in, to get the bait inside, but once he gets inside, he can't get out again."

"Where do they put these traps?" asked Djuna. "Anywhere in the water?"

"Not just anywhere," said Billy. "You have to put them out in deep water, mostly out by the islands, two or three miles from here. The lobsters move around on the rocks away under the water. You see these stones that are fastened in each of these lobster pots? That's so the box won't float, but will sink down to the bottom, where the lobsters are."

"Then how can you find the box again, away under water?" asked Djuna.

Billy pointed at a pile of short, thick pieces of wood, heaped up near the lobster pots. Each one was painted red and white, and had a number or some letters painted at one end. But the paint was old and dry and peeling off.

"You see those?" asked Billy. "They're marker buoys. Before you sink a lobster pot under water, you fasten one of these markers to it with a rope, and the rope has to be long enough so that the marker will float on top of the water. Then, when you want to pick up the trap, you just haul the marker into your boat and pull the lobster pot up after it, from the bottom."

"What do those letters mean, painted on the markers?" asked Djuna.

"Oh, that shows who the marker belongs to," said Billy. "These are all marked 'P T,' you see. That stands for 'Phineas Truelove.' But old Phinny doesn't do any fishing, himself, any more. He just buys and sells whatever he can get from the fishermen—lobsters and fish and steamers, mostly."

"Steamers!" exclaimed Djuna, in surprise. "You mean steamships?"

Billy Reckless laughed. "I guess you've never been around this part of the country before," he said. "Steamers—that means clams that you steam, to cook 'em. Just wait till you try some! Gee, I could eat a bushel of 'em, any time! You dip 'em in melted butter, and, oh, boy, are they good!"

"How do you catch them?" asked Djuna innocently. "With a hook and line?"

Billy laughed again. "You don't catch them, you dig them," he explained. "You go out on the mud flats, at low tide, and dig them out with a kind of a spade, only it's more like a bucket on the end of a pole, really. We'll go claimin' someday, I'll show you."

"Gee, that will be swell!" exclaimed Djuna. "But where is this place, Low Tide? Is that anywhere near here?"

Billy Reckless stared at him in amazement. "Say, what are you talking about?" he asked. "Don't you really know what low tide is?"

Djuna shook his head. "No," he said. "You said the mud flats were at Low Tide, didn't you? What's wrong with what I said?"

Billy gave a whistle of astonishment. "Well, dog my cats!" he said. "You're the first person I ever heard of that didn't know what *tide* is! Come here, I'll show you! Come out here to the end of the pier with me. My goodness, it's time you knew!"

He started off down the yard, motioning Djuna to follow. The black terrier, Champ, had been busily gnawing away at one of the wooden markers lying on the ground and didn't want to leave, but got up when Djuna pulled at his leash.

They walked out on the pier, which, at that end, was so wide that Mister Truelove's little store was built on it, but Billy led the way past the store and along the narrower part of the pier, which was like a wooden sidewalk on stilts, stretching out fifty feet beyond the store. Djuna followed him till they came to the very end of it, wondering what Billy was going to show him.

At the end of the dock, Billy pointed toward the next pier, a little way off.

"There, look there!" he commanded. "See those posts the dock is built on? See how far the water is from the top of the dock? Pretty near six feet, I guess. Well, that means it's about low tide right now. Pretty soon the tide will change, and begin to rise. And by the time it's high tide, the water will be three feet higher than it is now. See that strip of beach over on the other side of the harbor? Well, after the tide comes in, you won't see any of it. It will all be under water. Same way with the mud flats where you dig for clams. Understand, now?"

"Of course," said Djuna. "But up where I live, there was a pond we used to fish on, and it never had any tide, so I didn't know."

"It must have been a fresh-water pond," said Billy. "This is salt water. The tide comes from the ocean."

He picked up a bit of wood lying on the dock and tossed it out into the water. After a moment it began to float slowly to the south.

"See that?" he asked. "Tide's still running out. That piece of wood may drift a couple of miles before the tide turns, and it begins to float this way again."

"How long will it be before the tide begins running in, instead of running out?" asked Djuna.

"It changes about once in every six hours," said Billy. "If it's high tide at six o'clock in the morning, then the tide will be running out until about noon. Then it changes and begins running in, and keeps that up for six hours, about, so that by six o'clock in the afternoon it's high tide again."

"Say, that's wonderful!" said Djuna, staring in fascination at the piece of wood floating steadily out to sea.

"What's so wonderful about it?" said Billy. "It's always been that way."

"Yes, but *I* never saw it before," persisted Djuna. "Why, it's just as though the ocean was breathing in and breathing out!"

"Well, you'll get used to it if you live around here," the thin boy chuckled. "Come on, don't you want to get that stuff for your dog?"

He led the way back along the narrow pier, towards Mr. Truelove's store, and Djuna followed him, though he was still deep in thought about the silent magic of the tide.

Old Phineas Truelove's store was built on a wide wooden platform at the edge of the water, on posts that stuck up above the platform so that boats could be moored to the posts when the fishermen brought fish and lobsters to sell to Mr. Truelove. Floating in the water, alongside the platform, was an enormous box built of heavy wood, with only the top above water. It was about fifteen feet long and six feet wide. A square hole, about two feet square, in the middle of the big box, was covered with a wooden lid.

"What's that for?" asked Djuna, as they came opposite the floating box. "Is that a float, to dive from, when you go swimming?"

Billy shook his head. "That's a lobster pound," he explained patiently. "Ever hear of a dog pound, where they put dogs? Well, this is a lobster pound, where they put lobsters, live lobsters. Mister Truelove keeps them in there until somebody comes along to buy them."

"Gee, I'm going to ask Aunt Patty if we can have one!" exclaimed Djuna. "I never ate any lobster. Are they good?"

"Are they good?" echoed Billy, rolling his eyes. "I'll say they're good!"

Then he looked at Djuna in surprise.

"Hasn't Aunt Patty had lobster for dinner since you got here?" he asked. "*She* doesn't have to buy 'em from Phinny Truelove—she catches them herself!"

"She does?" exclaimed Djuna. "I didn't know that! No, we didn't have any lobster last night, we had lamb chops. I only got here last night, you know. She hasn't said a word about lobsters. Does she really catch them herself?"

"Sure," said Billy. "She's got a string of lobster pots out off Sixpenny Island and Haypenny Island."

"Where's that?" asked Djuna.

Billy pointed off to the south, across the water.

"Oh, they're about three or four miles out," he said. "They's so small that you can't hardly see them from here. She owns 'em."

"Gee, she must be rich!" exclaimed Djuna, impressed by the thought that anyone could actually own two islands.

"She isn't rich," said Billy. "They aren't worth anything much. You couldn't live out there. They're just rocks. All they're good for is to fish from."

"How does she get out to them?" asked Djuna, wonderingly.

"With a boat, of course," said Billy. "That's her boat over there."

And he pointed to a small but sturdy motorboat tied to the next pier. Djuna could read the name painted at the bow of the boat—PATAGONIA.

"That's a funny name for a boat!" exclaimed Djuna. "Patagonia—why, that's a place down in South America! It's in my geography."

"Well, maybe it is," said Billy. "But that isn't where she got it. It's her own name."

"What do you mean?" asked Djuna.

"I mean Patagonia," said Billy. "That's Aunt Patty's name. Patty—that's short for Patagonia. I guess she named her boat after herself."

Djuna stared at the boat with admiration. Its sides were scratched and scarred, and a good deal of its paint had peeled off, but it looked reliable.

"Gee, I'd like to go out in that boat!" he exclaimed. "Do you suppose Aunt Patty would take us along, next time she goes?"

"Sure, she will," said Billy, confidently. "She took me, one time. Why don't you ask her?"

"I will, right away!" said Djuna. "As soon as I buy Champ's biscuits."

They hurried into Mr. Truelove's store. Mr. Truelove was sitting at one end of the counter, smoking his pipe and reading a newspaper. He was an old man, with a little gray beard under his chin that made him look like a billy-goat. He stood up slowly and asked them what they wanted.

Djuna told him that he wanted to buy three cans of

dog food and a box of dog biscuits, and Mr. Truelove hunted around the shelves until he found them.

"Haven't ever seen you before, have I, young man?" he asked, looking at Djuna sharply. "'You live here in Stony Harbor?"

"I just came here," answered Djuna. "I'm going to stay at Aunt Patty's, I mean Mrs. Tubbs' house, for a while."

"Oh, so you're going to stay at Aunt Patty's, are you?" asked Mr. Truelove. "Well, you couldn't stay at a better place, nohow. Mrs. Tubbs is a mighty fine woman."

"Yes, sir," said Djuna.

He paid Mr. Truelove for the packages, and the old man put the money away carefully into a leather bag full of coins.

"Yes, sir, everybody thinks a heap of Aunt Patty, here in this town," Mr. Truelove observed. "Well, come in again, young man."

Billy Reckless had been standing at the other end of the counter, with his eyes greedily studying the things for sale in the glass case. He beckoned to Djuna.

"Look at this," he said. "These big rubber bands. Five cents apiece, that's what they cost. Someday I'm going to get a couple of them and make me a slingshot."

"Gee, you could make a dandy slingshot with them, couldn't you?" said Djuna. "But, look, let's go ask Aunt Patty about the boat, shall we?"

They left the store and had gone only a few steps when Billy suddenly stopped short. "Oh, shucks!" he exclaimed. "I can't go with you! I just remembered I promised my dad I'd stay home this afternoon. He has to go over to Yessank, and there won't be anybody to take care of our boat yard except me."

"Boat yard?" exclaimed Djuna. "Have you got a boat yard?"

"Sure," said Billy. "My dad rents out boats. Say, why don't you come over this afternoon? We could go out with Aunt Patty, maybe, some other time."

"Well, maybe I will," said Djuna. "I'll see what Aunt Patty says."

"See you later, then," said Billy Reckless. "So long!"

"So long!" said Djuna. "Come on, Champ!"

"Come on, Alberto!" said Billy, whistling to his imaginary dog.

And Djuna, followed by his black Scotty, went one way, while Billy, followed by a dog that could be any color that Billy pleased, went the other.

2. What Champ Found in the Attic

DJUNA FOUND Aunt Patty Tubbs putting plates and knives and forks on the kitchen table for their lunch.

"Gracious, I was beginning to think you were lost!" she exclaimed, smiling.

Djuna had so many things to tell her that he hardly knew where to begin. So he tried to tell her everything at once.

"I met a boy named Billy Reckless," he said breathlessly. "He's got a dog, only it isn't a real dog, it's a dog he made up, and he calls him Alberto. We had an awful lot of fun. You can make Alberto do all sorts of tricks, Aunt Patty, because all you have to do is to *think* he's doing the trick, and he does it, see? You know Billy Reckless, don't you?"

"Yes, I know Billy," said Aunt Patty. "But I didn't know he had a dog like that. Sounds sort of crazy to *me*, I must say."

But her eyes twinkled and Djuna knew she didn't mean what she said.

"So we went to Mister Truelove's store together," Djuna hurried on, "and Billy showed me the lobster pound, and I saw your boat, Aunt Patty! And Billy says there are two islands out there that belong to you, and, please, could I go out to see them with you, the next time you go?"

Aunt Patty smiled at the way the words came tumbling out. "Why, of course, Djuna," she said. "And I think we had better go out there this very afternoon. I didn't get out there at all, yesterday, what with getting this house dusted and cleaned, before you got here, and I don't want to let my lobster pots go too long without looking at them. Yes, I guess we had better go as soon as we've had a bite to eat."

"Oh, hurrah!" shouted Djuna. "When do we eat?"

"Right away," said Aunt Patty. "As soon as I steam these clams."

Into a deep stewpan she put the clams, a whole quart of them, from a paper bag. On top of them she poured one cupful of water and then set the pan on the stove.

"Is that all the water you need?" asked Djuna, watching it all.

"Yes, their own juice will make two cupfuls, besides the water," said Aunt Patty. "You'll see."

"Where did you get the clams?" asked Djuna. "Did you dig them, out at your island?"

"Oh, my, no," said Aunt Patty. "I got them at the fish market, while you were out. I haven't gone clammin' for years, myself. It's awful hard work, and I'm too old for it. But folks go out to my island–Haypenny Island, I mean, the other one hasn't got any clam flats–and dig for 'em, every once in a while. I don't mind, as long as they don't meddle with my lobster pots at Sixpenny Island."

"Do they ever do that?" asked Djuna.

"Well, I don't know that they have," said Aunt Patty, "but some folks are mean enough to do anything. There really isn't any way of telling, unless you catch 'em at it."

She lifted the lid of the stewpot and peeped in. A delicious fragrance of clam broth filled the air.

"They're done, I reckon," she said. "All the shells have popped open."

She ladled out a generous heap of the steaming clams on each of their plates, and then poured from the pot a cupful of the clam juice for Djuna and one for herself. She had already placed salt crackers, a dish of coleslaw, two big glasses of milk, and two saucersful of melted golden butter on the table.

"Now," she said, taking her chair, "let's be thankful!"

Djuna had never tasted anything so delicious as those clams, dipped in the melted butter. By the time they finished, Aunt Patty and he had heaped up a small mountain of empty clam shells on their plates.

"Oh, boy!" said Djuna, with a sigh of satisfaction. "Am I glad I came to Stony Harbor!"

When Aunt Patty had washed the dishes and put them

away, she went into the woodshed beside the kitchen door and closed the door behind her. When she came out again, Djuna could hardly believe his eyes. She had changed her clothes, and was wearing overalls, a pair of short rubber boots, and a man's coat, together with an old straw hat with a wide brim, which she had tied under her chin. She looked just like a man.

"These are my lobstering clothes," she explained, noticing Djuna's look of surprise. "It's liable to be wet work, lobstering is."

"Are we going to start now?" asked Djuna excitedly. "Can Champ go with us."

"I'm afraid not," said Aunt Patty. "Better put him in the woodshed, I guess."

So Djuna locked Champ up in the woodshed, giving him some dog biscuits to chew on for comfort, and they set off for the dock where Aunt Patty's boat was tied. But first Aunt Patty got two long oars that were leaning against the woodshed and lifted them to her shoulder. She held the oars with one hand, and with the other she carried a jug that she had filled with fresh drinking water.

"You can bring that empty bucket along, Djuna," she said. "We'll get some bait at the fish market."

"What are the oars for, Aunt Patty?" asked Djuna. "I thought your boat was a motorboat."

"It is," said Aunt Patty. "But it's got an awful old engine in it, and if the engine ever breaks down, we'll need the oars to get home with. It's never broken down, yet, but I'm taking no chances."

At the fish market, Aunt Patty asked Mr. Steptoe, the man who had the market, if he had any lobster bait to spare. Mr. Steptoe filled Djuna's bucket with scraps of fish that he was going to throw away, and then they went on to the boat.

When they got to the ladder at which her boat was tied, Aunt Patty put down the things she was carrying and climbed carefully down the ladder to the deck of the boat. Djuna handed the oars and the jug and the bucket of bait down to her, one by one, and then scrambled down to the deck of the boat, eagerly.

The *Patagonia* was only sixteen feet long and seemed to be almost half as wide as it was long. The engine, which had been covered with an old piece of canvas, was in the stern cockpit. The wheel was up forward, enclosed in a little house. All the space between the wheel and the engine was taken up by a wooden well, in which the lobsters—if they caught any—were to be put. Aunt Patty put the jug of water and the bucket of bait in a locker under the stern seat.

In a few minutes Aunt Patty got the engine started, and then Djuna helped her unfasten the mooring lines, keeping one rope loosely around the mooring post on the dock until Aunt Patty gave the word. When she had taken her place at the wheel, she said, "Cast off!" Djuna hauled the rope on board, Aunt Patty started the propeller, and the *Patagonia* moved slowly but grandly away from the dock.

As they passed the next pier, which was the one where Mr. Phinny Truelove had his store, they saw him standing at the end of his dock. Djuna waved to him, and Mr. Truelove waved back and shouted "Good luck!"

Aunt Patty, with her eyes fixed steadily ahead, steered the *Patagonia* among all the boats anchored in the harbor and headed out to sea. Djuna, standing beside her, looked excitedly around, for this was the first time he had ever been so far from land. Everything seemed different. Even the houses on shore looked different now, as their boat chugged slowly past them. It was like seeing houses in a foreign country. They all stood in a neat, orderly row, looking very small at that distance, and at the end of their line was a house with stone walls and a low tower. That was the lighthouse at the end of the Point, Aunt Patty said. The wind blowing toward them brought the smell of the ocean, a wonderful salty smell. Soon the stubby little *Patagonia,* leaving the harbor behind, began to rise and fall gently with the gentle waves rolling in from the sea, and sometimes a larger wave would slap against the *Patagonia's* nose and send a splatter of spray flying past them.

"Would you like to steer for a while?" asked Aunt Patty suddenly.

Djuna's heart gave a jump. "*Would* I!" he exclaimed eagerly. "Could I, really?"

Aunt Patty showed him how to manage the wheel and to hold the boat on its course, and Djuna quickly learned the knack of steering.

They were heading for the two little islands that belonged to Aunt Patty. She pointed in their direction, but they were so far away and so low that at first Djuna could not see them. They seemed, when he first saw them, only a gray line above the water. But one of them became more and more distinct as they came closer, and in a few minutes Djuna could see that at one end of it there was a large, bare rock, as high as a house.

"Now you can see the islands," said Aunt Patty. "They call that rock Eagle Rock. And now you had better let me take the wheel again. There are a good many rocks under water, around here, and if you don't know the channel you are liable to hit one."

She slowed the boat down as she took the wheel, and they moved forward very cautiously.

"Where is the other island?" asked Djuna. "I can see only one."

"That low ground in front of you is Haypenny Island," said Aunt Patty. "From here, it looks as if it were part of Sixpenny Island, but it isn't. There's a narrow channel between them."

As the *Patagonia* crept nearer to Sixpenny Island, going slowly around it, Djuna caught sight of a piece of wood floating upright, the end sticking up several inches out of the water. It was painted red and white.

"Oh, look!" he exclaimed, pointing at it. "What's that?"

"That's one of my lobster-pot marker buoys," said Aunt Patty. "Now we'll see what we've caught."

She steered the boat over to it and shut off the engine just as she reached the floating stick. Leaning over the rail, she lifted it in, and then began hauling at the light rope that was fastened to its lower end. Djuna, standing beside her and watching with excitement, soon saw the lobster pot appear at the other end of the rope, as it rose slowly through the clear water. The rope was dripping and so was the box, as Aunt Patty lifted it on deck with a final heave. As she had said, it was wet work. But Djuna gave a squeal of joy as he saw two large lobsters through the slats of the box, waving their big claws threateningly.

"They're good ones," said Aunt Patty with satisfaction. "They'll weigh all of a pound apiece."

"But I thought lobsters were red, Aunt Patty," said Djuna. "These are dark green. Aren't they ripe yet?"

Aunt Patty laughed. "All lobsters are dark green until they're cooked," she said. "It's the boiling water that makes 'em turn red."

When she had taken them out of the lobster pot and dropped them in the box-like wooden "well" in the middle of the boat, she fastened some fresh bait in the lobster pot, taking it from the bucket, dropped the lobster pot overboard again and tossed the red and white marker, with its rope, after it. Djuna watched the lobster pot sink slowly to the bottom, weighted down by the stones in it, until it disappeared from sight and only the marker was left floating to show where it could be found.

"There!" said Aunt Patty. "Now we'll go on to the next one!"

She started the engine up again, but by the time it began to chug again, the boat had drifted several feet away from the floating marker.

"What's making us move?" asked Djuna curiously.

"That's the tide current," answered Aunt Patty. "It runs a little faster, going out between these two islands, because the channel is so narrow. It carries things along with it. See those gulls over there? They're watching for any scraps of food they can find floating in the tide. They're always around here at this time of the tide."

Djuna had already noticed the big gray and white sea gulls which were circling back and forth over the narrow strip of water separating the two islands. Now and then one of them would make a sudden swoop downward and pick up a bit of floating seaweed, or anything else that looked as if it might be good to eat; and usually two or three other gulls would chase after the first and try to take it away from him. They were fun to watch.

Aunt Patty steered the *Patagonia* past the entrance to the channel and continued on around the edge of Sixpenny Island, keeping in the deeper water off shore and stopping the boat whenever she came to another of her lobster-pot markers. One by one, they hauled up the lobster pots, and although a few of them were empty, most of them had trapped one or two lobsters. By the time they had finished, both Aunt Patty and Djuna were pretty well soaked with water that had dripped from the lobster pots as they lifted them in and out of the boat. But, scuttling around in the bottom of the boat, safely under cover, were fifteen fine big lobsters!

"We can't eat *that* many, can we?" asked Djuna, wonderingly.

"Mercy, no!" exclaimed Aunt Patty. "We'll keep out a couple for our dinner tonight, and I'll sell the rest to Mr. Truelove. He's got plenty of customers for 'em."

As they sailed on around the islands, Djuna glanced at them longingly, thinking to himself what fun it would be to land on them and explore them. The smaller one, Haypenny Island, had no trees on it. Only a few low bushes and some long marsh grass grew on the middle of it. High above the bushes towered the big bare rock which Aunt Patty had said was called Eagle Rock. But on the other little island, he could see the walls of a small wooden cabin, whose roof timbers were outlined against the blue sky. Most of the shingles were gone from the roof. Big lilac bushes grew around the deserted cabin. Djuna wondered how long it had been since anyone lived there. But he saw that Aunt Patty was too busy with the lobster pots to talk, so he didn't bother her with any questions.

"Sixpenny Island!" he thought to himself. "What a funny name! I guess it's because it's so small, and almost round, like a penny."

When the last lobster pot had been dropped overboard, with its marker buoy floating to show how it could be found when they came back the next time, Aunt Patty turned her boat around and headed its nose for Stony Harbor. The engine chugged away steadily, the blunt bows of the boat scattered the spray, a fresh breeze blew from the southwest and ruffled Djuna's hair, and Djuna took deep breaths of the cool salty air. In half an hour they were back at the dock; but before they tied the boat, Aunt Patty steered it slowly alongside of the big floating box, the lobster pound, in which Phinny Truelove kept the live lobsters for sale. She stopped the engine and shouted for the storekeeper, and soon the old man came out of the store and to the dock, where he stood looking down at them with a grin on his face.

"Well, what luck did you have?" he asked.

"Count 'em yourself, when you take 'em out," retorted Aunt Patty. "You can put a dozen of 'em in the pound, and the rest I'll take home with me."

Mr. Truelove climbed down the perpendicular ladder that was fastened to the dock, stepped on board the floating box, and came over to the boat. With a heavy leather glove on his hand, he fished out a dozen of the lobsters one by one from the hold of the boat and dropped them into the opening on top of the lobster pound.

"All good big ones," he said. "Guess I'll have to allow

you twenty cents apiece for 'em, Aunt Patty. That makes two dollars and forty cents I'll credit you with. That all right?"

"That's right," Aunt Patty nodded. "Now, if you'll just rubber the other three, I'll take them along for our supper. I clean forgot to bring any rubbers with me."

Djuna wondered what on earth Aunt Patty meant by saying that she had forgotten her rubbers, when she was already wearing rubber boots. But before he could ask, he found out what she meant. Mr. Truelove fished a handful of strong rubber bands from his pocket. Then he picked up one of the lobsters. It waved its big claws around and tried its best to pinch Mr. Truelove's fingers. But he deftly snapped one of the rubber bands over each claw, and that finished the lobster's attempt to pinch. The claws of all three lobsters were quickly fastened in this way, and although their legs still moved around angrily, they were helpless to do any harm. Aunt Patty thanked Mr. Truelove. A vigorous shove sent her boat across the narrow strip of water to the other dock, and there she and Djuna climbed out.

Carrying the three squirming lobsters in the big brown paper bag which Mr. Truelove had supplied, Aunt Patty and Djuna hurried on home. Djuna's first care was to let Champ out of the woodshed in which he had been locked up. Champ jumped all around him, wild with joy. It took him ten minutes to quiet down enough to be given his dinner.

In the meantime, Aunt Patty put some water on the stove to boil, in a big pot, and started to get dinner ready. While she was taking down some salt and pepper from the pantry shelf, she noticed that her jar of mayonnaise was almost empty.

"Djuna," she said, "would you mind running down to Mr. Truelove's store and getting a jar of mayonnaise? I think we'll need more than there is here, for the lobsters."

"Sure!" said Djuna. Taking the money she handed him, he called to Champ and they scampered off together to the wharf. As he hurried into the store he saw that Mr. Truelove was waiting on another customer, so he stood quietly waiting by the counter until Mr. Truelove finished what he was doing.

The customer was a man Djuna had never seen before, but as Djuna had not been in Stony Harbor long enough to know much about the village, he supposed the man had always lived there. He was dressed in a summer suit of light gray cloth, and wore a fine straw Panama hat, jauntily perched on his thick curling black hair. He was not very tall. His hands and face were very dark, almost like a Spaniard's.

"Well, now, let's see," Mr. Truelove was saying, "them overalls will be two dollars and twenty-three cents."

The man took out his wallet and handed Mr. Truelove a twenty-dollar bill.

"That the smallest ye got?" said Mr. Truelove. "Well, never mind, guess I can change it, but I know I ain't got but seven dollars in paper."

He reached into the iron safe behind the counter, brought out the leather pouch in which he kept coins, and untied the string around it. Fishing around in it, he brought out five coins, and then took two one-dollar bills and a five-dollar bill from his pocketbook, and pushed all the money across the counter.

The man picked up one of the coins and looked at it curiously.

"Haven't got any more like this, have you?" he asked, turning it over in his dark fingers and looking at both sides of it carefully.

"No, sir, that's the only one I've got," said Mr. Truelove. "Only one I ever saw, far as I can remember."

"Do you remember who gave it to you?" asked the man.

Mr. Truelove rubbed his chin. "No, can't say that I do," he replied slowly.

The man looked at him for a moment, and then laughed. "Well, if you can't, you can't," he said pleasantly. "But if you happen to run across any more of them in the next few days, let me know, will you? My name's Patina. I'll be stopping at the Harbor House for the next few days. Good-bye, sir."

He picked up the rest of his change and the bundle that Mr. Truelove had put on the counter and strolled out, giving Djuna and Champ a friendly smile as he passed them.

"Now, son, what can I do for *you*?" asked Mr. Truelove, as he tied up the leather bag again and put it back in the safe.

Djuna told him, got the jar of mayonnaise, paid for it, and hurried home. He was feeling especially hungry, after the afternoon's fishing trip, and he was anxious to learn what lobster was going to taste like.

Aunt Patty had already put the three lobsters in the boiling water before he got back, and in a few minutes she announced that they were cooked.

"Why, look!" exclaimed Djuna, as she took them out

of the pot, "they were dark green when you put them in, and now they're bright red!"

"That's what always happens," said Aunt Patty, with a twinkle in her eye.

"I think one apiece will be enough, plenty," she added. "I'll put the other in the icebox, and we'll have a cold lobster salad for lunch tomorrow."

Then she showed Djuna how to crack the hard shells of the other two, so that the white meat could be easily taken out with a fork, and soon they sat down to dinner. Djuna thought he had never tasted anything so delicious as that lobster, along with ears of fresh corn, covered with melted butter.

When they had finished supper, Djuna gave a sigh of contentment.

"My gollies, that was marvelous!" he exclaimed.

After playing around the yard with Champ for a while, Djuna decided that he had better write a letter to Miss Annie Ellery, to tell her what a nice time he was having, and about Billy Reckless and his wonderful dog, Alberto, and the sail out to Sixpenny Island, and how he had helped Aunt Patty haul up the lobster pots. But when he asked Aunt Patty if she had any paper to write the letter on, she looked bewildered.

"My sakes, now what did I do with that writing paper?" she said. "I had some, somewhere, but I hardly ever write a letter. Let's see, what did I do with it? Seems to me, I put it away up in the attic. You just wait a minute, I'll go up and see."

Djuna decided he would like to see what was up in the attic, too, so he followed Aunt Patty up the narrow stairs. Champ had the same idea, so he followed Djuna. They made quite a parade.

The floor of the attic was bare, but all around the edges, close to the walls, which sloped inward to the ridgepole of the little house, were boxes and bundles that Aunt Patty had stored up there. There were only two windows in the attic, one at each end, but both of them were open. Outside one of the windows, Djuna could see the branches of a big elm tree, almost touching the house.

"I think I put that paper in the sea chest," said Aunt Patty, as soon as she had got her breath after climbing the stairs. She pointed at a big wooden box, with wooden handles at each end, that stood close to the sloping ceiling. "Help me pull it out, Djuna, so I can see."

Together they dragged the box out into the middle of the floor, and Aunt Patty lifted the lid. Djuna noticed that on the front of the chest was painted the picture of a sailing ship, and, under it, the letters, "B. G."

"This sea chest belonged to my great-grandfather," said Aunt Patty. "His name was Benjamin Greene. That's a picture of his ship, the last one he commanded. He was drowned in a storm off Cape Hatteras."

"Was the ship wrecked?" asked Djuna, staring at the picture of the ship.

"No, it got home safe," said Aunt Patty. "Captain Greene was the only one lost. He had been washed overboard."

She rummaged around in the sea chest, which was filled mostly with folded blankets, on which powdered camphor had been sprinkled, to keep the moths away.

From beneath the blankets she pulled out a small cardboard box labelled, "Writing Paper." She opened it.

"No, that's not it," she said disappointedly. It contained only a small bundle of old letters, and she put it down on the floor beside her. Hunting still further in the sea chest, she found what she wanted—the package of blank paper.

"Here it is!" she announced triumphantly. "I was sure I put it here."

She closed the lid of the sea chest and stood up.

"Now let's push this back," she said. But Djuna looked around the attic.

"Where's Champ?" he said.

Champ had disappeared. But just then they heard him scuffling and snuffling around somewhere behind the boxes against the wall. He had trotted into the narrow space behind the other boxes and bundles and was having a fine time investigating the tunnel.

"Come out here, Champ!" commanded Djuna, getting down on his hands and knees to see where the dog had gone.

Champ came out reluctantly. There was dust all over his black whiskers.

Djuna shooed him on down the stairs and then helped Miss Patty push the big sea chest back into place against the wall.

"Oh, I forgot to put those letters back in!" exclaimed Miss Patty, noticing the package of old letters still lying on the floor. "Well, never mind, I might as well keep them downstairs. I've forgotten what's in them, but if they're not worth saving any longer, I might's well throw them away."

"Shall I shut these windows before we go?" asked Djuna, hurrying over to the one nearest him.

"No, never mind," said Aunt Patty as she started downstairs. "I always leave them open in hot weather. It gets too stuffy up here if I shut 'em."

So Djuna followed her downstairs.

By the time he had finished writing his letter to Miss Annie Ellery, the sun had gone down, and it was beginning to get dark. It wasn't long before he began to yawn, and Aunt Patty said she guessed it was time for him to go to bed, because he had had a very busy day.

"Can Champ sleep up in my room?" asked Djuna. "He might get lonely, out in the woodshed by himself."

"Why, yes," said Aunt Patty. "Take him along if you want to."

In a few more minutes Djuna was sound asleep in his room, with Champ curled up on the floor, under the bed.

But in the middle of the night Djuna suddenly woke up. He didn't know what had awakened him, and for a minute he couldn't think where he was. The room was pitch dark. He sat up in bed. Then he heard Champ moving around in the dark. He whispered to him, and Champ jumped up on the bed and began to try to tell him something.

Just then Djuna heard a distinct thump on the ceiling just over his head.

His heart jumped. What could it be?

Champ wriggled in his arms, trying to get free. Djuna held him tight, while he listened, hardly daring to breathe.

But everything remained silent, and finally Djuna decided that he had been dreaming. "You'd better get down now, Champ," he whispered. "Go on back to sleep."

He lifted Champ down to the floor, but instead of going back under the bed Champ made a dash for the open door, turned the corner, and went rushing up the stairs to the attic, making all sorts of noise.

"Oh, dear!" groaned Djuna. "He'll wake Aunt Patty!"

And he did. Djuna heard her stirring around in the next room, and the scratch of the match as she lighted an oil lamp.

Djuna found his sneakers, slipped them on and went out into the hallway.

"I'm awfully sorry, Aunt Patty," he called out. "But we heard a noise up in the attic and I couldn't stop Champ from going up there."

"Well, I declare!" exclaimed Aunt Patty. "You probably heard some mice running around up there. But I guess you'd better keep your dog outdoors in the woodshed, after tonight. Here, take this lamp and get him out of the attic, and let a body get some sleep."

"Yes, Aunt Patty," said Djuna meekly, feeling very much ashamed of his dog's noisiness. He took the lamp and started up the stairs.

As he reached the top, he could hear Champ scuffling around in the darkness, and then heard him bark. He sounded as though he were over by the window.

"Keep quiet, Champ!" he commanded. "Come here!"

Much to his relief, Champ obeyed at once and came trotting over to him, emerging from behind a pile of boxes near the window. His long whiskers almost hid something he was carrying in his mouth. At first glance, Djuna thought he had found an old bone.

"What have you got there?" asked Djuna, sharply. "Give that here, right away!"

He put the lamp on the floor and reached down to take the thing out of Champ's mouth. Champ resisted a little, but finally let go.

It wasn't a bone, at all. It was something that looked a little like a broken doorknob.

Djuna couldn't imagine what it had been made for. It seemed to be a smooth roundish stone, not quite as big as a tennis ball. It was almost white, or very light brown, but it was spotted with blotches and specks of light cinnamon-brown and gray. Its whole surface was polished very smooth, and it glistened in the lamplight. It wasn't exactly round, but was shaped more like a small football. To one end of it was fastened a thick blunt screw. But the queerest thing about it all was that on top of the other end of the spotted stone there was fastened what seemed to be a bird's foot—a foot with four toes, each toe ending in an enormous claw. These claws, carved out of black stone, clutched the spotted white ball tightly.

Djuna turned the strange object over and over in his hands, wondering what it could be. It certainly wasn't a doorknob, but, he decided, it might have been used for the knob of a bureau drawer.

"Oh, well," he said at last, "I'll ask Aunt Patty what it is, tomorrow. You go on back to bed, now, Champ!"

Champ led the way down, his stubby tail wagging.

3. The Man Who Sat Down on Nothing

"HEAVENS TO Betsy!" exclaimed Aunt Patty next morning, as she stood looking at the strange "doorknob" which Djuna had found in the attic, turning it over and over in her hand. "I don't believe I've seen this thing since I was a little girl! But I remember it, all right. Seems to me my Ma told me it was part of Gramma's umbrella—the head of it. Anyway, 'tain't worth anything now. Might as well throw it away, Djuna."

"May I have it?" asked Djuna eagerly.

"Why, certainly," said Aunt Patty, smiling. "But what you want it for, goodness knows. The junk that boys collect beats all!"

Djuna looked at it again, thoughtfully, before he put it in his bureau drawer.

"Was your grandmother a very big woman?" he asked.

"Mercy sakes, what a question!" exclaimed Aunt Patty, startled. "No, she wasn't, she was a little bit of a thing. I never saw her, she died long before I was born, but I remember my mother telling me that *her* mother hardly came up to her shoulder. That was Gramma Greene, of course. What made you ask?"

"Oh, I don't know," mumbled Djuna. "I just wondered. Look, may I go and mail my letter to Miss Ellery, and then go to Billy Reckless' house? He said maybe we could go sailing together."

"Go ahead," said Aunt Patty. "You know where the post office is? It's at the end of this street, next to the Harbor House. You'll find Billy's house right near there, down by the wharf. You can't miss it."

"What's the Harbor House?" asked Djuna.

"Oh, that's a sort of hotel, for summer folks mostly, and travelin' men, but mighty few ever stops there. It don't amount to much."

Djuna whistled to Champ, who had been waiting for him at the kitchen door, and they set off. As they went around the corner of the house, Djuna noticed a long ladder lying on the ground, close to the house and right under the open window in the attic. He stopped, looked at it closely, and then went on down the street.

Near the end of the street of little white houses he found a store with the words "Post Office" in the window, and mailed his letter there. As he came out, he noticed three men talking to each other at the door of a shabby-looking building. Over the door was a sign reading, "Harbor House," but the paint had peeled off so much that it was hard to read it. He recognized one of the men as the man he had seen in Mr. Truelove's store, the day before, and who had called himself Mr. Patina. But to Djuna's surprise Mr. Patina was now dressed in overalls, instead of the neat gray suit he had worn before. Djuna had never seen the other two men. Their faces, which were sunburned, looked a good deal alike, and both were dressed in wrinkled blue canvas trousers and blue shirts. Mr. Patina was standing with his back to Djuna, and was bareheaded, and Djuna was sure he had never seen such glossy black hair as he had.

Just as Djuna passed them, on his way to Billy's, he heard Mr. Patina say, "Well, suppose we sit down and talk this over."

One of the two other men said eagerly, "Okay, mister," and took a step backward toward the wall of the hotel. Without looking around, he began to sit down. Djuna was utterly surprised, because there wasn't any chair there. But he wasn't as surprised as the man was. A look of complete astonishment spread over his face as he kept on going down, and landed on the ground with a bump. The other man said angrily, "Watch yourself, Bonehead!" but it was too late. He had already landed.

He scrambled to his feet, still looking bewildered. "My gosh!" he said, rubbing himself, "there's allus been a bench there!"

Djuna hurried around the corner, trying hard not to laugh. The last thing he heard was the reproachful voice of the man who had sat down on nothing. "Why didn't you *tell* me they moved it, Harvey?" he was saying.

Billy Reckless waved to Djuna as soon as he came in sight. He was standing on the little wharf by his house. Several rowboats were moored alongside the dock, and three or four more were pulled up on the gravelly beach. At the end of the dock was a small motor fishing boat, not much larger than Aunt Patty's and much dirtier. No one was on board it. Farther out, two small sloops were moored to buoys, their noses pointed toward the incoming tide.

"Hi, Djuna!" yelled Billy. "You're just in time! I was just coming up to your house to look for you! Want to go sailing?"

Djuna quickened his steps. "Oh, boy!" he said as he reached the dock, "you should have seen what *I* just saw!"

Billy grinned when Djuna told him about the man who had sat down on a bench that wasn't there. When Billy heard that the other man had called the first one a bonehead, he said:

"Oh, I know who that was! That's Harry Bohnett, only everybody calls him Bonehead, because he's always doing dumb things like that. The other one is his brother Harvey. That's their boat out at the end of the dock. They don't live in Stony Harbor, but they come over here once in a while. I don't like them, either of them."

"Why not?" asked Djuna.

"Oh, they're always too fresh. But, look, I don't know whether we ought to take your dog along with us or not. Maybe you'd better take him home before we start, don't you think?"

Djuna's face fell. He didn't want to leave Champ behind again, as he had had to do the day before. He thought fast.

"You're going to take Alberto along, aren't you?" he asked. "Champ won't take up any more room than *he* does."

Billy laughed. "You win!" he said. "Get him into the boat, but watch out and don't let him fall overboard. Make him stay up in the bow, along with Alberto."

But Champ objected to climbing down the short ladder that led to the landing float, and Billy finally had to go down first, and take Champ when Djuna lifted the dog down into his upstretched hands.

"Aren't you going to put up the sail now?" asked Djuna after they had all settled themselves in the boat. He was crouched in the bow, keeping one hand on Champ's collar.

"No, not till I push her out from all these other boats," said Billy, picking up the oars. "It's easier, if we wait till we get out where there's more room."

Pushing away from the float, he rowed the boat out to the outermost of the two anchored sloops and came up close beside it, in the lee of the sloop. He carefully put the oars in the bottom of the boat, while Djuna held onto the side of the sloop. Then Billy put a rope through a ringbolt on the afterdeck of the sloop and handed the loose end of it to Djuna.

"Hang on to that until I get the sails hoisted," he commanded, "and don't let go till I yell, 'Cast off!' Just watch what I'm doing, this time, and next time you can help a lot."

From the locker in the tiny forepeak, he pulled out two bundles of canvas, the sails.

"Now," he said, "wait until I hoist the mainsail and get back to the tiller. When I yell, 'Cast off!' let go that rope and make sure it doesn't get tangled up in that ringbolt on the sloop. Then grab *this* rope, the jib halyard, and hoist away on it until the jib is up as high as it will go; then fasten the halyard around this cleat, coil up the rest of it and stow it under the seat. We'll be moving backwards by that time, because the wind is blowing toward us, but don't worry. I'll be swinging the boat's bow around to starboard, so be sure to get your head over to the other side, to port—that's to the left, you know. Think you remember all that?"

"I think so," said Djuna, a little anxiously. "First I let go, when you say so, then hoist the jib, then keep over to port. Is that right?"

"Swell!" said Billy. "You've got it! Okay, let's go!"

Standing close to the mast, he began hoisting the main halyard, and the mainsail began to rise, little by little shaking out its folds. As the wind filled it, it began to flutter, and the boat woke into life, tugging at the line by which Djuna held it tethered, as if it were a live colt trying to get free.

When the mainsail had risen to the top of the mast and had become a white fluttering triangle, Billy deftly made the halyard fast to a cleat, and hurried back to the stern seat. Glancing at the mainsheet to make sure that it would run free, without tangling, and that the jib-sheets were close at hand, he took a firm grip on the mainsheet and tucked the tiller under his right elbow.

"Cast off forward!" he yelled.

Djuna, who until that moment hadn't taken his eyes from Billy, let go the rope as if it burned him, and watched it anxiously until its end slid through the ring-bolt on the yacht's deck and dropped into the water. He began to haul it in.

"Never mind that now!" yelled Billy. "Let it drag! Hoist your jib!"

Djuna, dimly remembering that he must stay on the lefthand side of that sail, did as he had been told, and reached for the jib halyard. He fumbled a little before he got the rope unfastened from the cleat, then began to haul on it. Up, up, went the fluttering little triangle. The wind filled it, and it began tugging to the right as Billy had said it would.

Djuna looked anxiously upward and saw that the jib had been hoisted as far as it would go. Breathlessly, he fastened the rope to the cleat, and to his surprise found that his hands were shaking with excitement. Looking toward Billy, he saw that Billy was working just as busily. He had already pulled the starboard jibsheet taut and made it fast, and now he was pulling the main-sheet in toward him, hand over hand, while he still held the tiller firmly under his right arm.

Djuna glanced over his shoulder. They had already drifted fifty feet backwards, away from the yacht. It seemed for a fraction of a second that the boat was standing still. Then, slowly, it began to move forward. Another moment, and Djuna heard the softest, merriest sound he had ever heard. It sounded as though the boat itself were chuckling, laughing to itself. "Glug, glug, glug!" it said. "Chuckle, chuckle, chuckle!" The sound was the sound of the little waves slapping against the bottom of the boat as it moved forward. Yes, they were moving!

He looked around, and burst out laughing. Champ had wiggled himself into the little sail locker, to get himself out of harm's way! His hairy face looked out so mournfully that Djuna couldn't help laughing.

Billy was pulling the end of the mainsail boom in closer to him. The boat leaned a little, with the growing push of the breeze on the sail. The chuckling noise under the bow grew louder as the boat moved faster.

"Haul in that bowline!" yelled Billy. "Coil it up, and then come back here, if you want to!"

Djuna stowed away the dripping rope that had been dragging in the water and then made his way cautiously back, to take a seat in the bottom of the boat beside Billy. It was a grand day. They were well out into the harbor now. The houses on shore were getting farther and farther away.

"Like it?" grinned Billy, as Djuna sat down beside him.

"*Do* I!" exclaimed Djuna. "Gee, this is swell!"

As the breeze grew stronger, the boat went faster, cutting its way swiftly through the rippled surface of the water. Djuna began to feel more confidence and to notice the direction in which the boat was sailing. It was heading southwest.

"Where are you going now, Billy?" he asked curiously. "Aren't you going to go out to Aunt Patty's islands right away?"

"Sure," answered Billy.

"Well, then, why don't you go that way?" asked Djuna, pointing south. "They're out there, aren't they? Seems to me we went that way, when I was in her motorboat."

Billy laughed. "Sure, you did," he said. "But then you weren't in a sailboat. A sailboat can't sail right straight toward the wind. This wind is blowing north, so we can't sail straight against it. We have to go zigzag. We can sail southwest for a while, and then we have to put the boat over and sail southeast. We zigzag like that until we get there. That's what you call tacking."

"Oh, is that the way?" said Djuna, a little puzzled. "And what do you do when you put the boat over? Does that mean you upset it?"

"My gosh, no!" laughed Billy. "That just means turning the rudder, so that the boat turns. I'll tell you, before I do. I'll yell, 'Coming about!' And when I yell, you duck your head as quick as you can, or else you'll get a whack on the head from the boom—that's this pole the sail is fastened to. You see, when I turn the boat, the wind hits the sail from the other side, and makes it swing across the boat, and, believe me, you have to duck under it mighty fast!"

In the next mile, Billy "tacked" twice, each time showing Djuna how it was done, and Djuna began to feel that he was learning something about sailing. Suddenly they heard the noise of a motorboat coming from behind them. They looked around. The motorboat was heading toward them, and traveling twice as fast as they were.

"That's Harvey Bohnett and Bonehead," said Billy, glancing back at them. "I hope they don't come too close, or they'll shake the mast out of this boat. We've got the right of way, though, because we're under sail. They're supposed to go astern of us."

But they didn't. As they came rushing up, instead of turning and going behind Billy's boat, Harvey Bohnett swung the wheel so that their boat circled in front of Billy's, throwing up a wall of water that made Billy's boat rock dangerously. As they tore past, the two brothers laughed and waved a mocking salute.

"You see what I meant when I said they're always doing something fresh?" exclaimed Billy indignantly, as he fought to keep the boat from rocking too violently. "They think they're awful smart!"

"Gee, they might have upset us!" exclaimed Djuna, staring after the motorboat as it rapidly drew farther and farther away.

"Oh, they wouldn't dare to!" said Billy scornfully. "They know my dad would knock their ears off if they got too fresh. Besides," he added proudly, "it would take more than that to upset *this* boat!"

Champ sent a defiant bark ringing across the water after the two men.

But both boys were too busy in handling their boat to waste much thought on the Bohnett brothers just then. Djuna had never realized before how much there was to learn about sailing. He had had a mistaken notion, like other people who had never sailed a small boat, that there would be nothing to do except sit in the boat and let the boat do all the work. Now he found that there was never a second in which he did not have to be alert and busy—especially when steering, when one had to watch the sails every instant to see that they were catching the breeze as they should. His respect and admiration for Billy Reckless, who seemed to know everything there was to know about a sailboat, increased with every minute.

For another full hour they sailed on, steadily drawing nearer to the distant islands, and Champ began to grow very restless, squirming around in the limited space of the forepeak, and occasionally venturing to put both forepaws on the gunwale and peer across the water as if he were Christopher Columbus himself, in black whiskers.

When they had come so close to the two islands that they seemed about to pass them, Billy sent the boat sharply into the wind. The sails flapped uselessly and the boat drifted slowly. Quickly the two boys lowered the sails, and then Billy got out the oars and fitted them into the oarlocks.

"Now watch," he said, "and I'll show you our secret harbor."

It was "slack" tide, by now, and the water was scarcely moving. Billy rowed the boat into the narrow channel between the two islands, and then, pulling hard on his left oar, he sent the boat shooting into a still narrower channel which cut through the low sandy beach of Haypenny Island. This inlet passed between two rocky boulders which were so close together that there was barely room for the boat to pass. But when they had passed these rocks, Djuna saw to his surprise that the inlet widened a little, forming a tiny cove which was hemmed in on three sides by the curving base of a big rock which towered high above their heads. They were completely hidden from view, and floated motionless on the surface of the dark still water of the pool.

"Oh, boy!" exclaimed Djuna, looking around him in wonder. "What a swell secret harbor!"

"Isn't it a dandy?" asked Billy. "Only trouble with it is that you can't stay here more than a couple of hours. When the tide runs out, the whole cove is empty, and if your boat got caught in here, then you'd have to wait till the tide filled it up again."

"Well, gee, it's a wonderful harbor, anyway," insisted Djuna. "Just room enough for one boat, and that's all!"

"You could get a bigger boat in here," Billy pointed out, "but not two at a time, and that's a fact. Come on, let's go ashore, shall we?"

Using the oars as paddles, they pushed the boat close to shore, scrambled out, and fastened it to some sturdy bushes which grew at the foot of the rocks. Champ gave a jump which landed him safely on dry ground, and at once gave a bark of relief. Immediately he started on an exploring trip, and the boys followed.

"Aren't you going to call Alberto?" asked Djuna innocently.

Billy shook his head. "We'd better leave him on board, to guard the boat," he said seriously. "You stay there, Alberto, do you hear?"

There was no answer, but Billy seemed satisfied. "He won't let any stranger put his foot on board," he said proudly, as they started on.

First of all, they climbed the rock. Its slope was steep, and if it had not been for the little bushes growing in the cracks and seams of the great gray boulder, which gave them handholds and footholds, it would have been a difficult job. It was fully twenty feet high. But when they had got to the flat top of Eagle Rock, they gave a shout of joy.

Stretched out in front of them was the immense blue sea, its wind-ruffled surface glittering in the sun. So big it was that Djuna thought it must be the ocean itself. Far in the distance, wisps of trailing smoke came from passing steamships, so far away that the ships themselves could not be seen. White sea gulls perched upon the rocks at their very feet. The salty breeze ruffled the boys' hair.

"This is the first time I ever saw the ocean!" exclaimed Djuna.

"Well, you haven't seen it *yet*," said Billy calmly. "This is just what they call the Sound. But it's really part of the ocean. It joins the ocean over there, off that way." And he pointed eastward.

"Aunt Patty told me her great-grandfather was the captain of a ship," said Djuna, with his eyes fixed on the farthest blue horizon. "Do you suppose it was a steamship? Do you suppose he crossed the ocean?"

"They didn't have steamships that long ago," said Billy. "He must have been captain of a square-rigger, a sailing ship; probably a whaler. There used to be a lot of whaling ships here at Stony Harbor, my father says. Sure, he crossed the ocean, if his ship was a whaler. Whaling ships used to sail all around the world, my father says."

The nearest point of land they could see to the eastward was a very narrow strip of white sandy beach that extended westward from the mainland, toward the islet on which they were standing. It was about half a mile from them, across the water.

"What is that beach called?" asked Djuna, pointing at it.

"That's Pinetree Point," said Billy. "There's a Coast Guard station over there. The channel from here to Pinetree Point is called Pinetree Channel. That's where the old whale ships used to go, when they started off from Stony Harbor to go to the South Pole, almost, to hunt for whales."

"Pine tree?" repeated Djuna. "I don't see any pine tree over there. Was there a pine tree there once?"

"Not that I ever saw," said Billy. "It's just sand and marsh grass—hey, look at there! Look at that big bird!"

Djuna followed his excited upward gesture just in time to see a tremendous dark-feathered bird, three times as big as any crow, diving straight down from the sky overhead. It hit the water with a splash of spray and rose again almost instantly, its broad wings flapping. In its claws was a big fish, shining silver as it struggled.

"That's an eagle!" exclaimed Djuna. "Look, he caught a fish!"

"That isn't an eagle, that's a fish hawk!" said Billy, just as excitedly. "I saw one last summer! An osprey, that's what it is! Boy, look at him climb!"

Fascinated, they watched the big bird rising swiftly, the fish firmly clutched in its claws, up, up, into the air.

Then, they never knew exactly from where, but from far overhead, a dark thunderbolt shot downward.

Out of the blue sky it fell, at terrific speed, straight down toward the fish hawk which was flying upward.

Seeming twice the size of the fish hawk, it was a bird that dropped out of nowhere, down from unknown heights, hidden by the sun.

Almost too late, the osprey saw its danger. Desperately, it changed its upward flight and darted off to one side, still clinging to the fish it had caught.

Its attempt to save its food was useless. The huge bird above it instantly checked its downward dive and, with a single stroke of its mighty wings, swerved and followed the frightened fish hawk. For a few seconds the two great birds zigzagged back and forth, the smaller one desperately trying to escape, while the boys held their breath in excitement, and then the hunted osprey opened its claws and let the fish drop. Its pursuer instantly dived for the fish and caught it in mid-air, before it had time to strike the water. Then, beating its huge wings, it came flying straight for the boys!

The two boys gasped. "Down!" whispered Djuna. They dropped to the ground. The low bushes on top of the great rock were just high enough to hide them. They lay flat, their hearts beating, scarcely daring to breathe. There was a swish of great wings, and they peered through the bushes just as the mighty eagle alighted at the other end of the flat rock, thirty feet away.

It was an eagle, and no mistake. As its claws, still clutching the fish, touched the rock, it shook its mighty wings above its head, spreading them as wide as a man's outstretched arms, then lowered them to its sides, and gave a scream of triumph. "Cac-cac-cac-cac!" it screamed, the cry ringing out over the water. The boys had only time to glimpse its dark-brown body, almost black, and its snow-white head, its fiercely gleaming yellow eyes and its cruelly hooked beak, when there was a scuffling in the bushes beside them, and Champ came snuffling up the slope.

The shaggy little black terrier saw the eagle at the same instant that the great bird turned its head and, for the first time, saw the intruders on its lonely rock. Champ growled and started straight for the angry eagle. With one impulse, both boys rose to their knees and flung themselves on him, tackling him before he had got past them. "Stop it, Champ!" panted Djuna, as they struggled to hold him back.

But the eagle had no intention of losing the dinner he had already seized. Again his great dark wings flapped, and he launched himself into the air angrily. Up and up he rose, with each beat of the mighty wings. The boys, on their knees now, watched him with open mouths. Only Champ, still struggling to get at him, hurled defiance after him.

Higher and higher rose the majestic bird, and the boys' heads tilted farther and farther backward as they watched him in awed silence, until at last the sun blinded them and they could see him no more.

Only then did they find their voices. "Gosh!" said Djuna, in an awed whisper. And, from Billy, came the equally reverent whisper: "Oh, boy, was he *somethin'!*"

4. The Stolen Nest Egg

"THAT WAS a *bald* eagle," announced Billy Reckless importantly, as they got to their feet and gave up trying to watch for the eagle any longer.

"Bald?" exclaimed Djuna. "Why, his head was all *covered* with feathers!"

"Sure," said Billy, "but didn't you see how white they were? That shows he was pretty old. I suppose they call them bald because if you saw one a good way off he might look as if he was bald. Did you see the white feathers in his tail, too? Gee, wasn't he close! I'll bet hardly anybody ever sees one as close as we did! He must have been so set on getting that fish that he never even noticed us until Champ came along! Didn't he act as if he owned the place, though?"

Djuna nodded. "Well, they call this Eagle Rock, don't they?" he said. "Gee, do you suppose he has a nest here?"

Billy shook his head. "I don't think so," he said. "There aren't any trees here, and my father says they always nest up at the top of the highest tree they can find. He found one once, up on top of Lantern Hill. That's the highest hill there is around here, about twenty miles off that way. But that's the last time anybody ever saw one around here, I guess. They're awful scarce."

They walked over to the other end of the rock, where the eagle had alighted, but found nothing on the bare stone but a few drops of blood from the fish that the eagle had carried away with him. Looking down, across the narrow channel separating them from Sixpenny Island, they could look down on the deserted cabin over there. Its walls were half-hidden, because it had been built in a little hollow, but they could see plainly what was left of the roof. All the shingles had blown away in the winter winds, long before, and only the rafters were left. It was so near them that they could almost look down into the empty house.

"Bet you I can throw a stone inside the house before you can," said Billy.

He picked up a small pebble and threw it across the channel. It hit the wall of the cabin and bounced off.

Djuna's turn was next. He took careful aim and threw with an easy upward swing. The pebble curved in a gentle arc and disappeared inside the hut, falling between two of the rafters. They heard it thump on the floor.

"Shucks, I wasn't trying, that first time," said Billy. "Watch me now."

His second throw landed inside the cabin. "See?" he said. "It's too easy. Come on, let's go over there and see what's on that island."

Before they started to scramble down the rock, he pointed to the low ground that formed the rest of Haypenny Island. From the foot of the rock to the edge of the water, the tiny island was only about a hundred feet wide. Most of it was gravel, though there were a few small bushes and tufts of marsh grass here and there; but from the base of the rock to the beach stretched a low narrow mound which was almost buried in green ferns and bushes. From above, it looked like a wide green path, dividing the island in two.

"That's where you can get steamer clams by the bushel," said Billy, pointing to the beach. "The flats are under water now, but you can get all you want at low tide. Let's bring some shovels over someday and get some, shall we?"

"You bet!" said Djuna. "Look, you can see Stony Harbor from here! And, look, there's one of Aunt Patty's lobster-pot markers!"

The lobster-pot buoys, painted red and white, each one marking the position of a lobster pot under water, were strung out in a line close to the islands. Beyond them, looking across three miles of blue water, the boys could see the clustered little white houses of Stony Harbor, with the lighthouse tower rising above them.

"Well, come on," repeated Billy. "We'd better get our boat out of the cove before the tide starts running out."

They scrambled down to the secret cove, Champ at their heels, and found the boat floating safely at the end of its mooring line, though there was no sign of Alberto. Tumbling in, they pushed off. There was still plenty of water under them, but when they came to the channel between the two islands they found the tide moving gently toward the sea, and let the boat drift with it until they were clear of the shore. Then, hoisting only the jib, Billy worked the boat slowly around to the western side of Sixpenny Island, where they found the remains of a rickety pier, and there they landed.

Sixpenny Island was quite different in appearance from Haypenny Island. There were no large rocks upon it, although it was fringed with many sunken rocks, alongside of which the lobster pots were lowered. The roofless cabin was sheltered from the sea winds only by a ridge of gravelly soil. A few feet from its sagging door was a clump of tall dark-green lilac bushes, growing around some flat stones. Beside the stones stood an old bucket, to whose handle was attached a frayed rope. Going up to investigate, they found that the stones lay beside the mouth of an old well, lined with moss-covered stones. They tossed a pebble in and heard it splash.

They went on to the little cabin, whose unpainted walls were blackened with age. At one end, a brick chimney was still standing, though its bricks were beginning to crumble. The glass in the windows of the house had long since been broken, and the windows were boarded with planks nailed across them. The front door, before which was a large flat stone that served as doorstep, had swung inward on its one remaining hinge, and had wedged itself against the planks of the floor. Champ trotted in first, and the boys squeezed themselves through the doorway after him.

Looking up through the rafters, they could see the blue sky overhead. The oaken planks of the floor had rotted away in several places, from the rains and snows that had fallen on them year after year. There was a brick fireplace at one end of the room, where the chimney stood, and beside it stood a large iron kettle. On the floor, on each side of the fireplace, were great heaps of clamshells, whitened with age.

"For Pete's sake!" exclaimed Djuna. "Clamshells, right on the floor!"

"Oh, people used to come out here and camp, before the roof blew off," said Billy. "They would just eat clams by the bushel, and never bother to throw the shells outside."

"Didn't anyone ever live here?" asked Djuna. "There must have been *somebody* living here, once upon a time."

"Oh, sure," said Billy. "This was where Captain Tubbs lived before he married Aunt Patty. But he died an awful long time ago. My gosh, fifty years ago, I guess! Why, my father was just a little boy when Captain Tubbs died! He doesn't even remember what he looked like, exactly."

"Well, didn't anybody live here, after Captain Tubbs died?" persisted Djuna.

"I don't think so," said Billy. "I suppose Aunt Patty used to come out here, once in a while. But now she just comes out to 'tend to her lobster line. I don't think she ever comes on shore here any more."

"She didn't, when I was with her," said Djuna. "I

wanted to see what it was like, but I didn't like to ask her. We just got the lobsters and went home."

"Well, we can come out here in *my* boat any time we want," said Billy. "She won't care."

Champ had been sniffing around the corners of the room while they talked, as he always did in a strange place, but found nothing to interest him except an old rubber boot, which he pretended to gnaw at savagely. Litter of all sorts was scattered about the floor—a ragged old mattress, stuffed with straw; a broken oar; a rusty bucket; a tattered almanac.

"Well, come on, let's get out of here," said Billy. "No use looking at this old junk. We'd better be starting back. I'm getting awful hungry, and it's going to take us a couple of hours to get back, anyway."

"Me too," said Djuna. "Gee, I wish we'd brought something to eat with us!"

The homeward voyage was made in much less time than it had taken to sail out to the islands, because the breeze, which still came from the south, was now behind them and drove them along at a great rate. They no longer had to zigzag back and forth, tack after tack, as they had been obliged to do when "beating to windward," but flew steadily along, toward distant Stony Harbor. Djuna was surprised to find that the waves didn't seem so high now, and that their boat was gliding more quietly than before, even though it was moving faster. At first he thought this was because the wind had died down, but Billy insisted that it was just as strong as ever.

"It just *seems* quieter, because we're going with it, instead of against it," he explained. "See that boat over there, going the other way; see how the waves slap up against it? But it's really more dangerous to sail with the wind right behind you, if it's very strong, because if a big enough wave catches up with you from behind it might upset the boat. But this is just a *light* breeze. This isn't anything!"

They entered the harbor and glided past the village docks, one after another, until they came to the pier at Billy's house, where they tied the boat up, among the other little boats lying there. Before they left, Billy showed Djuna how to roll the sails up neatly and to stow them away in the little locker up in the bow. Champ had already jumped out on the landing float, and was waiting impatiently to be helped up the ladder to the top of the pier. They lifted him up, and then Djuna looked back at the little boat.

"Gee, that was swell!" he exclaimed. "Thanks a lot! Say, look, can you come over to my house this after? I've got something I want to show you."

"Sure," said Billy. "I'll be over soon as I get something to eat."

When Djuna got home, he found Aunt Patty had already put the lobster salad on the table, and between mouthfuls he told her excitedly about the big eagle and the fish hawk they had seen from Haypenny Island.

"My goodness!" exclaimed Aunt Patty. "I don't believe anybody's seen an eagle around here for I don't know *how* many years! But there used to be—"

She stopped suddenly, without finishing what she started to say, and Djuna was surprised to see her lips trembling. Tears began to trickle down her cheek. She reached hastily for a corner of her apron and wiped them away.

"Why, what's the matter, Aunt Patty?" stammered Djuna, quickly putting down his fork.

Aunt Patty sniffed and smiled. "Nothing, dear," she sighed. "Go ahead and eat your lunch. I was just thinking of something that happened a long time ago."

Her lips trembled again, and she got up and hurried out into the kitchen. Djuna felt very uncomfortable. He wondered if he had said anything that hurt her feelings. But he was sure he hadn't. He hadn't talked about anything except the eagle and the osprey, the fish hawk. Suddenly he remembered what Miss Annie Ellery had told him before she sent him from Edenboro to spend the summer with Aunt Patty:

"I'm dreadfully afraid Aunt Patty's in some sort of trouble. But don't bother her with questions. Just find out for yourself."

Yes, he thought, she certainly must be in *some* sort of trouble! What could it be?

Whatever it was, Aunt Patty managed to make herself seem as cheerful as usual when she came back into the room. She began talking about the visitors she had had that morning, while Djuna was away.

"I declare, I never had such a morning!" she exclaimed. "One person after another was here, a regular stream of 'em! You hadn't been gone ten minutes before Mr. Truelove knocked at the door. After he left, there was a junk dealer came along, said he wanted to buy old paper. An hour later, Cap'n Atterbury stopped in. Just before you got home, Emmy was here. She wanted some stamps. And the funny thing about it was that every last one of them wanted to go up to the attic! I had to go up and down those stairs till I was completely tuckered out!"

"Who is Emmy, Aunt Patty?" asked Djuna.

"Why, haven't you met little Emmy Lowry yet?" asked Aunt Patty in surprise. "She's a very nice little girl—Billy Reckless' cousin. I should have thought Billy would have taken you to see her. They live right next door to Billy's house."

Djuna shook his head. "He didn't say anything about her," he said. "What did she want stamps for?"

"For her stamp collection," Aunt Patty explained. "She thought maybe I would have some old letters with stamps on them that might be worth something, so we went up to the attic to look. But I couldn't find any. I wish you had been home. I didn't know where you put those letters we brought down from the attic last night, so I couldn't help her any."

"Oh, I put those letters in the top of my bureau drawer," said Djuna. "I was going to read them, but I forgot. But there weren't any stamps on them. There weren't any envelopes, even. But, gee, that's funny, that they *all* wanted to go up to the attic! What for?"

"Well, Phinny Truelove thought maybe I might have an old chair up there that I'd be willing to sell him. Said he needs a chair, and didn't want to spend money for a new one. So we looked around for one, up there, but the only one we could find had a broken leg. He took it along with him, anyway. Said he guessed he could mend it."

"Did he pay you anything for it?" asked Djuna.

"He gave me ten cents for it," said Aunt Patty. "He watches his pennies mighty close, Phinny does. Well, I was glad to get rid of it. 'Twasn't worth any more."

"What did the junk man want?" asked Djuna. "What kind of old paper?"

"Oh, anything," said Aunt Patty. "I didn't think there was anything he'd want, but he was so nice-spoken about wanting to see for himself that I let him look. All he found was a bundle of old newspapers. But he dragged them down, and carried them out to his wagon to weigh them. Gave me a nickel for them."

"What does he do with them?" Djuna asked.

"I'm sure I don't know," answered Aunt Patty. "I never saw the man before. Come to think of it, there hasn't been a junk wagon around here for I don't know how long. Well, and then old Cap'n Atterbury came along and took up some *more* of my time."

Djuna giggled at Aunt Patty's expression. "What did *he* want?" he asked.

"If I hadn't been so tired, going up and down those stairs, I'd have been glad to see him," said Aunt Patty. "But, no! What do you suppose he wanted? He said he was planning to write a piece about the old whale-ship days in Stony Harbor, and did I have any of the log books my great-grandfather Captain Benjamin Greene had kept on his whaling voyages. Well, I was sure I didn't, but I made the mistake of saying that if any of them were anywhere they'd be up in the attic. So nothing would do but he must go up there and look. We didn't find any, of course; just as I expected."

"What's a log book, Aunt Patty?" Djuna asked curiously.

"Why, that's the record book that a ship captain writes in, whenever a ship makes a voyage," she replied. "He puts down in it everything that happens, each day—how many miles the ship sailed, and what direction, and what the wind and weather was like, and if they saw any whales, and so on. But I don't know whatever became of Captain Greene's. He was awful disappointed, Cap'n Atterbury was."

Just then Djuna heard a whistle outside, and hurried outdoors, where he found Billy Reckless waiting for him.

When he got close up to Billy, he spoke in a low voice. "Say, listen," he whispered, "when we go into the house, don't say anything to Aunt Patty about that eagle and the fish hawk we saw."

"Why not?" asked Billy in surprise.

"Well, I told her about them," Djuna whispered, "and she almost started to cry. What do you suppose is the matter with her?"

"She did?" exclaimed Billy, in astonishment. "For Pete's sake! What's wrong with talking about an eagle? It wasn't our fault if we saw it, was it?"

"Well, I don't know, but, anyway, I guess we hadn't better say anything more about it while she's around," said Djuna. "Maybe she's scared of them, or something."

"Okay," said Billy. "But that's a funny thing to be scared of, when she didn't even see it. Gee, I'll bet she would have been scared if she'd been as close to it as *we* were! Did you ever see anything like those claws it had? Oh, boy!"

"Say, I've got something funny I want to show you," said Djuna. "Come on in and see if you ever saw anything like it before."

He led the way into the house and up the stairs to his own room. Opening the bureau drawer, he took out the queer-looking object that Champ had picked up on the floor of the attic—the smooth spotted stone held in the grip of a big bird's claw. Billy took it and stared at it.

"What is it?" he asked. "Where did you get it?"

"Well, Champ picked it up on the attic floor," Djuna said. "Aunt Patty says it was the top of an umbrella her grandmother used to have, the handle of the umbrella. But I don't see how it could have been. It's too big. Why, the stick of the umbrella must have been as big as a baseball bat, or this part here couldn't screw into it. And Aunt Patty said her grandmother was a little bit of a woman. She *couldn't* have carried an umbrella as big as that! And, look, what kind of a claw do you suppose that is?"

"Well, it's some sort of bird," said Billy, examining it more closely. "A rooster, maybe? I'd have said an eagle claw, right away, except that it isn't half as big as that eagle's claw. And what's it holding onto that egg for?"

"That's just what *I'd* like to know," said Djuna. "It's an egg, all right, but what kind of an egg? And what does it mean? It must mean *something!*"

"Oh, I don't think it has to mean anything special," said Billy carelessly, handing it back to Djuna. "Lots of umbrella handles are crazy looking, like that. What are you going to do with it?"

"Nothing," said Djuna putting it back in the bureau drawer. "I just wanted to show it to you, before I told you how Champ happened to find it. That's really the funny part of it. It was right in the middle of the night."

"What was?" exclaimed Billy, beginning to look interested.

"The noise." Djuna pointed at the ceiling overhead. "I woke up in the middle of the night, and I heard a thump on the floor, right up there. Then Champ barked and woke Aunt Patty up, and we went up to see what it was.

And there wasn't anything. But that's when Champ found the thing, there on the attic floor."

"A burglar!" said Billy, excitedly.

Djuna shook his head. "Oh, no, it couldn't have been," he said decidedly. "We took the lamp up there and looked around, and there wasn't anybody. I know what it was—it was squirrels. The window was open, and there's a tree right by the window, and they could have gone in and out, easy. That claw thing was probably lying on top of a box, and they knocked it off and it fell on the floor. That's all it was."

"Well, let's go up and look again," Billy urged. "Maybe we could find some footprints!"

Djuna laughed. "Squirrel footprints, that's all you'll find," he said. "Come on, though, if you want to. See for yourself!"

When they reached the attic, Djuna pointed out the corner where Champ had found the carved claw. Billy went over to it and began tugging at the trunks and boxes that stood along the wall.

"Let's see if there's a squirrel's nest behind here," he said. "Here, help me lift this trunk—it's awful heavy."

When they had made room behind the boxes, they got down on their hands and knees and crawled in under the sloping roof. Billy gave a cry of triumph. "Here it is!" he said. A good-sized hole had been gnawed in the lowest board, giving an entrance into the space between that board and the outer rafters. On the floor beside it were twigs and bits of paper.

"There must be mice in there, instead of squirrels," said Djuna. "Look how this paper has been chewed up, to make their nest out of!"

He picked up one of the scraps of paper, bigger than the others. It was a long, narrow strip, apparently the top of a sheet of paper, from which all the rest had been gnawed away.

"Why, it's got writing on it!" he exclaimed. "It's part of a letter!"

Backing out of the dark corner, he took the ribbon of paper over to the window and examined the writing closely. There was only one line, but the handwriting was crabbed and the ink was faded. At last he made it out:

"I have put the nest egg where it be."

Billy reached for it, as Djuna finished reading it. "Let's see!" he said eagerly. "*'I have put the nest egg where it be.'* What does it mean? Can you get any sense out of it? 'Where it be'—that isn't right. 'Where it *is*.' But that doesn't make sense, either."

"Don't you see the corner of the paper is chewed off?" asked Djuna. "That last word is torn in two. It was probably, 'I have put the nest egg where it belongs,' don't you suppose? I don't see any sense to that, either, do you?"

"No," said Billy, "and what kind of an egg is a nest egg, anyway? Do you know?"

"Why sure," said Djuna. "It isn't a real egg, it's a china egg. Mr. Johnson had some. Mr. Johnson is the farmer we used to get our eggs from when I lived in Edenboro. He had a lot of hens, and sometimes, when a hen didn't lay eggs, Mr. Johnson would put one of those china eggs in her nest, 'cause when a hen sees an egg in her nest it makes her want to lay another one. A nest egg is something to fool a hen with, see?"

"Is that what it is?" said Billy. "Well, then, whoever wrote this letter must have kept chickens. That's all there is to it! But what would he want to write a whole letter about it for?"

" 'I have put the nest egg where it belongs,' " repeated Djuna, staring at the ribbon of paper as if he expected it to say something else. "Where *does* a nest egg belong? Sometimes it belongs in a nest, but sometimes it doesn't. That's the silliest thing I ever heard of!"

Billy brightened up. "Oh, *I* know!" he said. "It's somebody that borrowed an egg from somebody else, and then put it back where it belonged! See?"

"I have put the nest egg where it belongs," said Djuna for the fifth time, in a sort of a singsong. "Well, maybe that's it. But it still sounds crazy to *me!*"

"It's the craziest thing I ever heard of," Billy agreed. "Borrowing an egg!" He giggled.

"I'll tell you what," said Djuna, thoughtfully, "we might see if we can find any of the rest of this piece of paper. If we could find the rest of it, it would show what it was about. Gee, I hope the mice didn't chew it *all* up!"

They picked up the rest of the tiny pieces of paper lying on the floor near the hole in the board, but it was no use. Not a single scrap had anything written on it.

"Oh, shucks!" said Billy, in disgust. "Let's go! It's awful hot up here."

"I thought you were going to look for footprints," said Djuna, teasingly.

"Oh, I was just fooling," said Billy. "Come on, let's get out of here."

When they were downstairs, they found Aunt Patty just getting ready to go out.

"Are you boys going to be around here for a while?" she asked. "I'm going out to do some marketing, but I won't be gone long."

After she had gone, the boys went outdoors, where they found Champ waiting for them, and sat down in the shade, on the grass. Billy noticed the long ladder lying on the ground at that end of the house. Then he looked from the ladder to the attic window above it, which was still standing open.

"You could put that ladder up and get into the window that way," he remarked.

"Sure," said Djuna, "but *I* wouldn't want to try it. That ladder is awful heavy."

"Then how can Aunt Patty lift it?" asked Billy.

"She doesn't," said Djuna. "It isn't hers. It belongs to the man that fixed the roof. It's been lying there for a week, she said, and he hasn't come back for it."

Billy looked up again at the open attic window.

"Maybe that's the noise you heard in the middle of the night," he ventured hopefully. "Maybe somebody climbed up on it and went away again before you saw them."

Djuna laughed. "I thought of that," he said. "But it couldn't have been that. Nobody has touched that ladder for a week."

"How do you know?" demanded Billy. "You haven't *been* here that long."

"Well, go look at it," said Djuna. "Just pick up one end of it. See how the grass has grown up over it? See how white the grass is, where the ladder was? You see?"

"Gee, I guess you're right!" said Billy admiringly, as

he examined the wilted grass on which the ladder had rested. "Of course it hasn't been moved!"

He came back and sat down again beside Djuna, looking very gloomy.

"Oh, pshaw!" he said. "As soon as you told me about hearing that funny noise in the attic, I thought maybe it was a burglar, and then we could have a lot of fun trying to get him arrested. We could have been detectives, and everything. But now, the way *you*'ve fixed it, there isn't *anybody* left to hunt for. Gee, I wish something would happen!"

"Well, I don't," said Djuna. "At least, I hope nobody ever steals anything from Aunt Patty. She's pretty poor, I guess, and she would feel awful if she lost any money. No, sir, *I* don't want any burglars around here, not one bit!"

"Well, for Pete's sake, you don't suppose *I* want Aunt Patty to get any of her old money stolen any more than *you* do, do you?" demanded Billy. "All I thought was—say, I'll tell you what let's do!"

He sat up, looking excited.

"Do you know what happened last night, Djuna?" he exclaimed. "After I went to bed, I heard Alberto barking out in the yard. I'm sure I did! He's got a very deep growl. I forgot to tell you, I changed him into a bloodhound yesterday."

"A bloodhound?" exclaimed Djuna. "Oh, boy!"

"Yes," said Billy, "so when I heard him growling I knew there were some robbers sneaking around our house in the dark, and then they ran off down the street. So I just said, 'Go get 'em, Alberto!' and he was on their trail just like a shot. He hasn't come back yet, so he must be following them about a hundred miles, I guess. That's the way a bloodhound does, he never quits. But maybe it would be more fun if we changed him into a police dog. We could, you know, easy. Shall we?"

"Well, that's all right," said Djuna, "but let's wait till we need him. It's too hot to do anything right now."

"Let's go swimming," suggested Billy.

"All right," said Djuna. "Wait till I tie Champ up in the woodshed."

"Why don't you bring him along?" said Billy. "Can't he swim?"

"Not very well," Djuna confessed. "His legs are too short. But he might as well come along, anyway. He can watch us."

They went back to Billy's house, and, after they had got into their swimming trunks there, Billy led the way to a beach on the other side of the village, where there was a bathing float anchored out a little way from the rocky shore. They swam and dived for a long time, while Champ amused himself by scrambling around among the rocks for a while, and then took a peaceful snooze in the sun. It was almost supper time when he and Djuna got back to Aunt Patty's house.

"Have you been gone long, Djuna?" asked Aunt Patty, as she set the table for supper.

"A couple of hours, I guess," said Djuna. "We went swimming. Gee, it was dandy!"

"I wondered where you were," said Aunt Patty. "I saw the front door open when I got home and I thought you were probably up in your room. But you weren't. That door wasn't open when you left, was it?"

"Oh, I'm sure we shut it when we went out," said Djuna. "When did *you* get back, Aunt Patty?"

"I didn't get back till ten minutes ago," said Aunt Patty. "Oh, well, I suppose it blew open. It always does, seems to me, if I don't lock it. I didn't expect to be gone more than a few minutes, when I started off to do my marketing. But then I decided to go and call on old Mrs. Atterbury. She's not feeling very well, lately, and I stayed and talked with her 'most all afternoon while Captain Atterbury took a walk. He can't leave her, you know, unless somebody comes to stay with her. Well, there's no harm done, but I suppose I ought to get that latch fixed. Someday, it will blow open when it's raining, and then things will get soaked. Oh, dear, when there's little enough money, it seems as though there was always something else to spend it on!"

"Gee, I'm sorry," said Djuna remorsefully. "Maybe I didn't shut it tight enough."

"Now, don't you worry," said Aunt Patty, kindly. "There's nothing in this house to steal, and nobody in Stony Harbor to steal it if there was. Get your chair, supper's ready. I should think you'd be terribly hungry, after all that swimming."

"I am," said Djuna. And he proceeded to do justice to everything on the table.

When supper was over and the dishes washed, Aunt Patty sat down in her favorite rocking chair in the front room, beside the little table on which stood the lamp, while Djuna went out to have a wrestling match with Champ on the grass. The wrestling match was interrupted by a chattering noise up in the tree beside the house, and Djuna looked up just in time to see a gray squirrel go whisking along a branch. When it reached the next branch it stopped and scolded at them some more, its feathery tail twitching in a rage. Champ rushed over to the foot of the tree and began barking furiously, but the squirrel only made faces at him. And just then Djuna heard Aunt Patty calling him.

He went back into the house to see what she wanted, and found her bending over in her rocking chair and pawing over the contents of her work basket, which she kept on the low shelf under the table beside the chair. Although she had pulled out most of the things in the work basket and they were scattered all over the floor beside her, she was still hunting for something in the basket.

"Djuna, have you seen anything of my darning egg?" she asked, in a perplexed tone of voice.

"Darning egg!" exclaimed Djuna, bewildered. "What kind of an egg is *that?*"

"It's a wooden egg," said Aunt Patty. "Don't you know what I mean?"

"I don't know anything about it, Aunt Patty," said Djuna. "I haven't seen it."

"Well, what on earth has become of it?" exclaimed Aunt Patty. "I had it here this morning, when I started to darn these socks. I had it here in this box, where I always keep it, and now I can't find it anywhere!"

"What does it look like?" asked Djuna.

"Like an egg, of course," said Aunt Patty. "Except, of course, it's wood. It's hollow, and it's light as a feather. My goodness, what *did* I do with it?"

And she pawed deeper into the work basket, fishing around among balls of yarn and bits of cloth, in her vain search for the missing egg.

Djuna picked up the little box in which, Aunt Patty said, she had kept the egg. It was about the size of a cigar box, but deeper, and was beautifully made, out of some sort of heavy, dark wood. It was lined with purple velvet. It looked like a jewel box.

"Gee, this is a nice box!" exclaimed Djuna, examining it admiringly. "What came in it, Aunt Patty?"

"Oh, I don't know," said Aunt Patty. "It was something that used to belong to my mother. I just keep odds and ends in it—needles and thread and buttons."

"What made all these funny-looking dents in the velvet?" asked Djuna. "All these rings, I mean. Was the whole box full of spools of thread?"

"I don't know, I'm sure," answered Aunt Patty. "It might have been, for all I know, when it was new. Mother had it before I was born. But, my goodness, I wish you'd stop asking questions and help me find that darning egg!"

Djuna hunted all over the room and even went upstairs to see if Aunt Patty had taken it up to her room, but it was not to be found anywhere.

"Well, that's certainly strange!" said Aunt Patty. "I can get another one, of course, down at the store—they only cost a nickel—but I can't get any darning done tonight. And these stockings certainly need it."

Sighing, she gathered up the things she had taken out of the work basket and replaced them.

"Now, what have I done with the lid of this box?" she exclaimed, looking around for it helplessly. "I declare, I must be forgetting how to remember anything!"

Djuna joined in the search and soon found the missing lid, lying on the mantel over the fireplace.

"How did it get *there*, of all places?" exclaimed Aunt

Patty. "Oh, I remember now—I was just going to put it away when that junk man knocked at the door and put it down there and forgot it. Well, I wish I could remember where I put that egg, too!"

Djuna glanced at the box lid as he handed it to Aunt Patty. It was lined, like the box, with purple velvet and on top of the lid, deep into the wood, were carved the words:

"HATCH & HATCH."

Djuna giggled. "That was a good place to put an egg, Aunt Patty," he laughed. "Maybe that wooden egg hatched out and walked off, all by itself."

Aunt Patty smiled. "Maybe so," she agreed. "Maybe I should have known better than to put it in there. But I'm so used to seeing that name on the box that I never thought of that. That was my grandmother's maiden name, Hatch was. Her father and his brother, her uncle, were in the importing trade, in Boston. Hatch & Hatch was the name of the firm. I suppose the box was something her father gave her, before she married Grandfather Hiram."

"What do you suppose was in it, when it was new?" Djuna said wonderingly.

"Gracious, I haven't an idea," said Aunt Patty. "Fancy soap, maybe. I haven't the faintest notion. Mother used to keep her spools of thread in it, so *I* do, too."

Djuna picked the box up again and looked at it thoughtfully.

"Gee, she must have had a lot of spools," he said, counting the round dents in the velvet lining. "Four crosswise and eight lengthwise—thirty-two of them! Gee, that's a lot!"

"Well, she sewed a good deal, mother did," said Aunt Patty. "She loved to sew. Can't say that I do, myself. I guess I was always too much of a tomboy, when I was a young one. If you don't learn to like sewing when you're a girl, you never do, I suppose."

Suddenly Djuna remembered the scrap of paper he and Billy had found on the floor of the attic that afternoon.

"Aunt Patty," he said, "did you ever raise chickens?"

Aunt Patty looked startled. "My goodness, what ever made you think of that?" she asked. "No I never did. Never had any room to, this yard is so small. But why?"

"Well, I found a piece of paper up in the attic—wait, I'll get it and show it to you." He raced off, ran upstairs, and was back in a jiffy with the scrap of paper on which the puzzling words had been written.

"Look!" he said, handing it to her. "What does that mean, Aunt Patty?"

Aunt Patty put her spectacles back on her nose and held the paper up to the light. "*'I have put the nest egg where it be,'*" she slowly read out loud. Djuna saw her fingers tremble. She handed the paper back to him, silently, and slowly got up out of her chair. Djuna saw with alarm that she suddenly looked old and pale and sick.

"I think I'll go to bed early," she said in a tired voice. "I—I don't feel very well. I guess the sun was too much for me today."

"But—but," stammered Djuna, worried by her looks, "I didn't—it isn't—is there anything wrong with what that says?"

"I'm sure I don't know what it means," said Aunt Patty,

firmly. "It's just nonsense of some sort, as far as I can see. Don't you think it's time for bed, Djuna?"

"Yes, ma'am," said Djuna hurriedly. "I'll just get Champ and put him in the shed. I won't be a minute."

He hurried out and called Champ. The squirrel had disappeared in the treetops, and Champ was wandering gloomily around the yard, pretending that he didn't care. Djuna put him in the woodshed and told him good night. By the time he got back, Aunt Patty had lighted the lamps upstairs and had come down again to close up the house. He told her good night and went up to his room; and soon he heard her come up and go to hers.

He opened the bureau drawer, and started to put the torn slip of paper carefully away in it, and then stood there in utter surprise.

The umbrella knob that he had put there—the carved egg, held in the carved claw—was gone!

Djuna's head whirled. It didn't seem possible. He remembered perfectly how he had put the umbrella knob back in the drawer after showing it to Billy. And now it had vanished!

He stood staring at the clean shirts and underwear that covered the bottom of the drawer, all put there so neatly by Aunt Patty. And he began to feel alarmed.

Somebody, he was sure now, had come into the house. How long had that front door been standing open, while no one was at home? Aunt Patty had been away, he had been away, not even Champ had been left at home. Anyone might have come in! To steal?

But the thing that worried Djuna the most was the queerness of it all. A wooden darning egg, that Aunt Patty had said cost only a nickel! An old umbrella knob, carved like an egg, that wasn't worth anything at all! It was all so queer that it made him feel dizzy. What sort of a person would come into a house and steal such things as that?

There could be only one answer to that question. A *crazy* person!

That was enough to make anybody worry, Djuna thought. A crazy person, who wants anything that *looks* like an egg, no matter what it's made of!

The words written on the torn slip of paper in his hand now began to worry him for the first time. *"I have put the nest egg where it be—"* What did it all mean?

Three different kinds of eggs, and all of them mixed up together. *Scrambled* eggs!

But Djuna didn't feel like laughing. He was wondering about the mysterious china egg, the nest egg, the one no one had seen. Aunt Patty had said she knew nothing about it. But was that what the unknown visitor had really been hunting for? Would he come back, to hunt for it again?

Djuna shivered. He undressed quickly, put out the light, and climbed into bed. But it was a long time before he got to sleep, because he could not stop wondering and wondering if the wooden darning egg, and the carved egg of the umbrella handle, and the china nest egg that somebody had put "where it belonged," had anything to do with each other.

5. A Murder

DJUNA HELD a long consultation with his faithful friend, Champ, the next morning, sitting out in the yard, where Aunt Patty couldn't hear them.

"I don't like the looks of things, Champ," said Djuna, gloomily. "I don't think it's funny, one bit, when things disappear the way they do. Somebody must have got into the house and stolen those eggs, but what for? They aren't worth anything. And that's just what worries me. Do you think whoever it was will come back again?"

Champ wagged his stubby tail, but made no answer.

"It seems to me you might help a little, at least," Djuna complained. "You're the only one I can talk to about it. I don't think I'd better tell Billy Reckless about it, because he'll probably just laugh at me, for thinking anyone would steal an old wooden egg, or an old umbrella handle. And I can't talk to Aunt Patty about it, because she might just get scared. But you'd better help, because I tell you right now I'm not going to forget it for one minute, until I find out what it's all about. You hear me?"

This time, Champ barked twice, and wagged his tail harder than ever.

"All right, then," said Djuna, "keep your eyes open. Now, you stay here with Aunt Patty, because I'm going over to Billy's house for a while."

But when he went into the house, to tell Aunt Patty where he was going, he was surprised to find her dressed in the old clothes she wore when she went out in her boat

"Oh, are you going out for lobsters?" he exclaimed "Can I go with you?"

"Of course," said Aunt Patty. "I was just going to ask you if you didn't want to come along. Would you like to ask Billy and Emmy if they want to come, too?"

"Gee, that would be fine!" exclaimed Djuna eagerly. "Shall I go and get them?"

"Run along and come right back," said Aunt Patty. "And be sure and tell Emmy's mother to tell Emmy to bring a jacket or a sweater with her. It looks like there was a good stiff breeze blowing in from off the Point this morning, and we may get good and splashed before we get back."

Djuna dashed off to Billy's house on the run and found Billy helping his father polish the brasswork of a beautiful big motorboat tied up at the wharf. Billy's father was just about the biggest man Djuna had ever seen. He had wide shoulders and big arms, and his face was very brown and jolly. His eyes were very bright blue and twinkled all the time, as if he had just heard a good joke.

"Hi, Djuna!" yelled Billy, waving at him. "Come on board!"

Djuna came forward shyly, when he first saw Billy's father, but as soon as he saw Captain Reckless' pleasant smile, he knew they would be friends.

"Hello, Djuna," said the big man, "where's that dog of yours?"

"Oh, he's home," said Djuna. "Aunt Patty sent me over to ask if Billy and Emmy can go lobstering with us."

"I don't know why not," said Captain Reckless. "I'll be glad to get rid of them for a while." He winked at Djuna.

"Come on, let's get Emmy," said Billy eagerly.

They hurried back to the house next door to Billy's and found Emmy sitting in the front room with her stamp album and a little pile of postage stamps that she was sorting out, and pasting into the book. Her back was turned toward them.

"Hey, Emmy, hurry up and come with us," said Billy. "We're going lobstering with Aunt Patty!"

Emmy jumped up from the table. "Well, wait till I put my stamps away," she said. Then she turned around and saw Djuna.

"Oh, excuse me," she said in a ladylike manner.

"What for?" said Billy. "Hurry up, Aunt Patty's waiting!"

"Aunt Patty says you'd better bring a sweater or something," said Djuna. "She says it's so windy we're probably going to get soaked."

"Oh, goody!" exclaimed Emmy, hopping up and down. "That's the way I like it!"

She gathered up the stamps and the stamp album as quickly as she could, put them away in the table drawer, and ran upstairs to get her sweater and tell her mother where she was going. Then all three of them hurried back to Aunt Patty's house, where they found her waiting for them, and they all started for the wharf where her boat, the *Patagonia*, was tied. On the way there, they stopped at the fish market to get scraps to bait the lobster pots with. The man at the counter looked at Aunt Patty in surprise.

"You're back early, aren't you?" he asked.

"What are you talking about?" replied Aunt Patty, with a puzzled expression. "I haven't been anywhere this morning. We're just starting."

"Didn't you go out before daylight this morning?" asked the fish man. "I went down to the wharf a little while ago, and didn't see anything of you."

"Well, why should you expect to?" retorted Aunt Patty. "I haven't left the house this whole morning."

"You haven't?" he exclaimed. "But your boat wasn't there at the wharf. I thought sure you must have made an early start."

"Not there?" exclaimed Aunt Patty, in amazement. "Of course it's there!"

"I'm just telling you what I saw, Mrs. Tubbs," said the fish-store man. "The boat isn't there. That's all I know."

Aunt Patty turned pale. Without another word she started off for the wharf as fast as she could go, and the three children hurried after her.

When they got within sight of the wharf, Aunt Patty stopped suddenly short and gave a cry of despair. Other fishing boats were tied along the long wharf, but the place where she always moored the *Patagonia* was empty!

With a groan, Aunt Patty hurried on. As she reached the wharf, she saw an old fisherman bending over a big net that he had spread out on the wharf to mend. She ran up to him.

"Where's my boat?" she panted. "John, where's my boat?"

The old man looked up. A look of complete surprise spread over his face.

"Why, Miss Patty!" he exclaimed. "Where did *you* come from? Ain't you been out?"

Aunt Patty's voice trembled. "Where is she?" she repeated wildly. "Where's the *Patagonia*?"

The old man got slowly to his feet. His mouth fell open, as he looked from Aunt Patty to the spot where her boat had been, and back again at Aunt Patty.

"Why," he said, "ain't you been out in her? What's become of her?"

"Who's taken her?" cried Aunt Patty. "Haven't you seen her?"

The old fisherman shook his head. "She was gone when I got here," he replied. "I didn't think nothin' about it. I supposed o' course you had gone out extra early, to look at your lobster line. There ain't nobody been here since I came, and I've been here since daylight. Had a heap o' mendin' to do on this net. No, sir, nobody's been here exceptin' Henry Steptoe come down here from his fish-house, few minutes ago, and I told him you must have gone out before daylight. Didn't see a soul, no, ma'am."

Aunt Patty turned quickly. "Billy," she cried, "run and

tell your father the *Patagonia* is gone! Ask him if he can help me hunt for her!"

"Shall I go with him?" asked Djuna excitedly.

"No, stay here with me," said Aunt Patty. "I might need you." She looked anxiously across the water of the harbor, which the wind was whipping into waves, but the *Patagonia* was nowhere in sight.

Aunt Patty walked out on the wharf and stood looking grimly at the two posts to which the *Patagonia* had been moored.

"You see?" she said bitterly, pointing at the posts. "The mooring lines are gone! They didn't just break–somebody unfastened 'em and took 'em, along with the boat!"

"That's a fact, sure's my name is John Jackson!" exclaimed the old fisherman angrily. "The thievin' scoundrels! I'd like to get my hands on 'em!"

Djuna leaned over the edge of the wharf and looked down at the water, which was only a foot or two below the planks on which they were standing.

"What are you looking at?" asked Emmy, peering over his shoulder.

"Oh, nothing," said Djuna, straightening up. "I was just thinking it's awful funny nobody heard them start the engine in the *Patagonia.* It made an awful noise, that time I went with Aunt Patty."

"They wouldn't have to start it," said Emmy. "They could just come up in another boat and tow it away, and not make any noise at all."

"Yes, I guess they could have," Djuna admitted. "But then *their* boat must have made some noise. We've got to ask everybody, I guess. Maybe *somebody* saw them."

Just then they heard someone shouting, and they all

looked around. A woman was hurrying toward them, down the path from the village.

"That's my wife!" exclaimed the old fisherman. "What's the trouble now?"

As she came closer, the woman waved her arm frantically. "John! John!" she shouted. "There's an empty motorboat driftin' in toward the Point! It's headin' right for the rocks!"

The old man waited to hear no more, but started on a run for the beach. Aunt Patty hesitated only a second.

"Emmy, will you stay here and wait for your uncle?" she gasped. "Tell him I'm awful afraid that's my boat. I've got to go and see!"

"Wait!" said Djuna excitedly. "Here they come, now!"

They all heard the roar of the motorboat in the distance, and, turning to look, they saw Captain Reckless' boat come tearing toward them at full speed, with Billy waving to them. He was waving something that looked like a piece of black cloth. In a few minutes more the boat had reached the end of the wharf and Captain Reckless shut down the motor and the boat glided up to them.

"What's all this about the *Patagonia* being gone?" shouted Captain Reckless as he came close. "We'll find her somewhere, don't worry!"

Aunt Patty choked back a sob. "Oh, that's just what I'm afraid of!" she said wildly. "There's a boat going ashore at the Point! Maybe it's too late!"

Captain Reckless stopped smiling. "Might be some other boat," he said. "But get in, all of you, and we'll get there as quick as we can. Look sharp there, Billy!"

Billy held the boat against the wharf while Aunt Patty and Emmy found seats in the cockpit, and as soon as

Djuna had jumped on board he cast off. Captain Reckless backed the boat around and headed for the harbor, gathering speed quickly.

"Look, Djuna," said Billy, pointing at the bundle of black cloth he had been waving as the boat first came toward the wharf, "I brought our swimming trunks along. I thought we might get a chance for a swim somewhere."

Djuna shook his head. "I don't think we'll have any time to go swimming until we find Aunt Patty's boat," he said. "Gee, I hope we do!"

As they passed the end of the pier and got out into the open water of the harbor, they began to feel the waves lift the boat up and down; and every once in a while a bigger wave would break against the bow and send a shower of spray flying past them. Aunt Patty and Emmy, sitting in the stern of the boat, were shielded from the spray; but Djuna and Billy, up in the bow, soon got well spattered.

"Gosh! we might as well get into our trunks right now!" exclaimed Billy.

They dived into the little cabin, quickly pulled off their shirts and shorts, and were back on deck in their swimming trunks in no time. The boat had just reached the mouth of the harbor and now they could see the wide blue Sound ahead, its surface dotted with white-capped waves which the wind was driving before it like a flock of white sheep on a blue pasture. In another minute they had passed the little hill on which stood the old stone lighthouse of Stony Harbor, and they could see the flat beach beyond the lighthouse, and the Point of the beach, surrounded by scattered rocks, half-buried in the sea.

A cry of despair burst from Aunt Patty's lips. She half-rose, then sank back and buried her face in her hands. "It's the *Patagonia!*" she sobbed.

They all stood horrified at what they saw. The empty fishing boat, Aunt Patty's sturdy old boat, had come to the end of her mysterious journey. She lay in plain sight, hardly a quarter of a mile away from them, lonely in her misery. She rolled a little, from side to side, as if struggling to get free. Once she lifted her head, then let it sink again, helplessly. A burst of white spray flew over her. And again she lifted her old head, slowly, bravely.

Billy's father gave a hoarse growl. "The cowards!" he muttered fiercely. "They've set her adrift to die! She's caught her stern on Knife Rock!"

But, just as he spoke, a higher wave rolled over the unseen rock. Its upward sweep, as it passed over the rock, lifted the heavy boat like a feather. It rolled onward. And the *Patagonia,* carried along with it, shook herself free from the rock and floated on!

"Look!" yelled Billy, exultantly. "She's loose! She's loose! Now you can get her, Dad!"

But Captain Reckless shook his head. "I can't do it, son," he said sadly. "She'll be in among all those other rocks in a minute. They're as thick as tiger's teeth in there. If I get in too close, we'll crack on 'em like an egg shell."

Djuna and Billy, Emmy and Aunt Patty, could not take their eyes away from the helpless *Patagonia.* With no one to steer her, the doomed boat turned as the mocking waves pushed her, this way and that, and she turned helplessly from one direction to another as if she were pleading for help. But no matter which way she turned, foot by foot she drifted closer to the rocks that waited for her. Djuna felt sick with pity for her. Blindly the old *Patagonia* floated on, swaying from side to side in the waves, like a wild deer that is crazed by terror and weak from wounds, feebly staggering to her death.

They were only a hundred feet away from her now. She was drifting sidewise. Djuna could see the anchor lying on the forward decking, the anchor rope coiled neatly beside it. Beyond her, terrifyingly close, the waves broke over the waiting rocks.

Djuna could bear it no longer. "Billy, I'm going to try to drop that anchor," he burst out. "Maybe that will stop her!"

And before Billy had time to answer, he plunged into the water.

Aunt Patty shrieked.

Djuna came up a dozen feet from the boat and shook the water out of his eyes. Turning his head, he laughed and waved his hand.

Captain Reckless' face was grim. "Billy, get that long coil of light line out of the cabin locker," he commanded sharply. "Quick! Aunt Patty, come here and take the wheel!"

As Billy dived into the cabin to get the rope, Captain Reckless turned the boat so that it faced the incoming waves, and slowed down the motor so that the boat stayed just where it was.

"Keep her just where she is," he commanded, as Aunt Patty took charge of the wheel. "We mustn't get any closer to those rocks!"

Then he took the coil of rope from Billy and hurried back to the stern of his motorboat, where a round life preserver was kept. Quickly he fastened one end of the light rope to the life preserver and fastened the other end to the mooring post at the stern.

"That boy's a swimmer," he muttered admiringly, as he jumped up again.

"You bet!" gasped Billy. "He can swim like a fish! Just look at him!"

Djuna was already halfway to the *Patagonia.* He was swimming strongly, and the waves were helping him on. Each wave lifted him and carried him closer to the drifting boat. But at the same time, each wave drove the helpless *Patagonia* closer and closer to the rocks. It was a race—a race in which the prize would be the life of the brave old boat. Djuna swam as he had never swum before.

Holding the coil in his left hand and the life preserver in his right, Billy's father swung his right arm with a mighty heave and threw the life preserver far out over the water. The rope uncoiled behind it as it flew through the air. The life preserver struck with a splash a few feet behind Djuna. But the waves began to carry it slowly after him, and the rope continued to uncoil as it moved, floating on the water.

"Look!" squealed Emmy, almost falling overboard in her excitement. "He's almost there! Swim, Djuna!"

Djuna was right beside the *Patagonia* now. Looking up, he saw her dripping sides swinging away from him. The deck was two feet higher than his head. It was out of reach. He kicked out desperately, found his fingers touching the slippery sides, and began to tread water, waiting for his chance. The next wave lifted him. He clutched at the coaming, gripped it, and came up as the boat rose on the wave. Swinging himself up with all that was left of his strength, he tumbled into the boat.

Panting, he picked himself up and ran toward the bow. If he could only anchor the *Patagonia,* she might still be saved!

But it was too late. Just as he reached the anchor, the wave that had lifted the *Patagonia* onward to the rocks dropped away from beneath her, and she struck on the rocks with a sickening thump that threw him to his knees.

Djuna struggled up, sick at heart because his effort failed. It was hopeless, now, to think that the *Patagonia* could be saved. He could hear her sides cracking as the next wave lifted her again and dropped her once more upon the pitiless rocks. Clinging to the wheelhouse rail, he worked his way back along the slippery deck toward the other end of the boat. As he jumped down into the cockpit, he suddenly saw something that made him stare in surprise. The oil lantern which hung from a hook in the ceiling of the tiny wheelhouse was burning! The wick glowed redly through the thick glass chimney, blackened with smoke.

Djuna hastily stepped into the wheelhouse, took the lantern from its hook, and blew it out. There was no time to wonder who had lit it or why it had been left burning there. His only thought was that if it was not put out, the *Patagonia* might catch on fire. Putting it back on its hook, he delayed no longer. Again he heard the *Patagonia* crunch against the rocks underneath her. Water was already bubbling up through the cracks of the cockpit floor. There was no time to lose!

As he scrambled across the cockpit, he heard Captain Reckless shouting at him and saw him pointing at the *Patagonia's* stern. "Under the stern!" shouted Captain Reckless. "Look under the stern!"

Djuna threw himself flat on the deck, and, hanging on carefully, peered over the gunwale. Right under his nose floated the life preserver, bobbing in the waves! He had been too excited to think of it!

He wasted no time, now. Slipping over the rail, he clung there until he had pulled the life preserver close enough, and then slid into it, until it rested under his armpits. He waved a hand. Captain Reckless began to pull in the rope, hand over hand.

It was a long pull, and a slow one. Instead of swimming with the waves helping him, as before, Djuna was now being pulled against them. The long rope was stretched tight as a bowstring. But, little by little, Captain Reckless' strong arms dragged him closer, and at last they reached down and hoisted him back to safety.

"Get his sweater for him, Billy," said the captain. "He's half frozen!"

"I'm all ri-ri-right," gasped Djuna. But his teeth were chattering. "I'm awful so-so-sorry! I thought maybe I could stop her from going on the rocks. But I c-c-couldn't!"

He bit his lip and hurried into the cabin. He couldn't talk about it any more.

Aunt Patty was still standing grimly at the wheel, her eyes fixed on the tossing waves ahead, intent on keeping the motorboat steady. Djuna was almost afraid to look at her. He felt ashamed of himself, ashamed to think he had failed.

But when he had got into his dry clothes and came out again, Captain Reckless was steering the motorboat, and Aunt Patty held out her hand to Djuna. She looked as though she were about to hug him, but she didn't. Instead, she shook hands with him, as if he were a man. Tears were in her eyes.

"You did your best, Djuna," she said. "I'll never forget that!"

"Oh, gee!" said Djuna, gulping. "Can't we do *anything*, Aunt Patty?"

"There isn't a thing we can do, now," said Captain Reckless, gruffly. "Nothing to do but wait for the wind to die down. Might just as well head for home. It won't be any too pleasant, just staying here and watching her take that beating. Shall we go, Aunt Patty? I'd better be getting things ready, so we can get busy as soon as there's a chance to get to her."

"Yes, let's go," answered Aunt Patty, in a hopeless voice. "I can't bear to watch it. If she has to go, I don't want to see it. I just don't want to."

Captain Reckless swung the boat's bow around, and headed homeward.

Djuna and Billy and Emmy stood staring back at the helpless body of the *Patagonia*, a tortured prisoner, as they drew away from her. A wave ran hissing over her, and she trembled.

"They've murdered her!" cried Djuna hotly. "That's just what it is—a murder!"

6. The Boat Lantern

DJUNA WAS burning with indignation, and he hardly said anything at all for the rest of the way back. Silently, he made up his mind that he would do his best to find out who it was that had treated Aunt Patty so cruelly.

Captain Reckless brought them up the harbor and slowed his boat down as he came near Mr. Phineas Truelove's wharf and store.

"I'll drop you off here, if you like, Aunt Patty," he said. "This is the nearest to your house. Then I'll take Billy and Emmy on home, and begin to get things ready to work on the *Patagonia*. It's high tide, now—nine o'clock. Low tide will be about three o'clock this afternoon. Then we can get out to her and see how badly she's damaged.

Yes, I guess we can wade out to her by two o'clock. Just you go on home and take it as easy as you can, Aunt Patty."

"Well, children, I promised to take you out lobstering," said Aunt Patty to Billy and Emmy, "but it hasn't turned out very well, has it?" She tried to smile bravely, but her voice trembled. "Never mind, we'll go some other time."

"Oh, gee, Aunt Patty, we're awfully sorry," said Billy. "Don't you worry—I'll bet my father can fix your boat up all right!"

"I'll do my best, Billy," said Captain Reckless.

Emmy just gave Aunt Patty a hug.

As Aunt Patty and Djuna climbed out on the wharf, Mr. Phinny Truelove came hurrying out of his store to meet them.

"What's all the excitement, folks?" he asked. "I see you all goin' off a hour ago, in an awful rush. Ain't been any trouble, has there?"

"The *Patagonia's* gone aground on the rocks, over at the Point," said Captain Reckless sadly.

Mr. Truelove looked horrified. "Why, that's terrible!" he exclaimed. "That's dreadful! She ain't smashed up bad, is she?"

"Don't know yet," said Captain Reckless. "I'm going to see what I can do as soon as the wind and tide goes down. Reckon you can come over there about two o'clock and give us a hand, Phinny?"

"I sure will!" said Mr. Truelove. "Miss Patty, I'm awful sorry! Indeed I am!"

Aunt Patty felt so badly over the loss of her boat that she could hardly speak, and quickly went on home.

When Captain Reckless and Billy and Emmy had gone on home in their boat, Djuna stayed on the wharf a while to talk to Mr. Truelove.

"Did you see anybody around the wharf where the *Patagonia* was tied up last night, Mr. Truelove?" he asked.

"I saw old Johnny Jackson over there this morning," said Mr. Truelove. "He was working on one of his nets. There wasn't anybody else over there. The boat was gone, but I didn't pay no attention to that, because I thought o' course that Aunt Patty had gone out in it. Hain't she got any idea how her boat happened to get loose?"

"It didn't get loose all by itself," said Djuna, miserably. "That's just the trouble. Somebody came and untied the ropes. It must have been before five or six o'clock this morning, because Mr. Jackson said he came to work on his nets then, and the *Patagonia* was gone when he came. You didn't see anybody around there last night, did you?"

"No, there wasn't a soul around that wharf, I'll swear to it," said Mr. Truelove, positively. "Leastways, there wasn't nobody there before midnight, up to the time I went to bed. If there had been anybody monkeying around there, I'd have heard 'em. No, sir, nobody could have started the *Patagonia's* motor without my hearin' them, and no boat could have come in there without my hearin' it."

"Were you here all the time?" asked Djuna. "I mean, you didn't go anywhere last night, did you?"

"I was right here, all the time," insisted Mr. Truelove. "I was settin' right here on the wharf. Harvey Bohnett and his brother come along in their boat about eight o'clock and they sat here with me, talkin' for an hour or so. The *Patagonia* was there, then, all right, tied up over there just as usual. I remember, because Harvey says to me, he says, 'It's a wonder the old lady don't give that boat of hers an overhaulin' once in a while,' and I says to him, 'Well, you're nobody to talk, Harve—*your* boat ain't nothin' to brag about, for looks.'

"So we set here, talkin', till after dark, and then the Bohnett boys went on to the Harbor House, and I went back into the store and listened to the radio till I went to bed. The *Patagonia* was still there when they left, there ain't any doubt about it. It's a mighty funny business! Only way to explain it, as far as I can see, is that Aunt Patty didn't fasten that boat as tight as she thinks she did. Ropes must have worked loose, some way. But I'm terrible sorry for Aunt Patty. Seems as though she's bound to have bad luck, all her life!"

"What do you mean?" asked Djuna, wonderingly. "Has she had a lot of other trouble?"

"She certainly has!" said Mr. Truelove, shaking his head sadly. "Had a hard time of it all her life. First of all, her father, Mr. Amos Greene, died when she wasn't but a little girl, and didn't leave her and her mother any money to amount to anything. Her mother had a hard time of it, making both ends meet. But she brought Patty up somehow, and Patty was a grown woman when her mother died. Then Patty married Bill Tubbs, who never was much good, as far as anybody could see, and then what does he do but fall off a tree and break his neck. Since then, Aunt Patty has had a mighty hard time of it. Bill Tubbs didn't leave her nothing but them worthless islands out yonder, and that shack he lived in, on Sixpenny. He was always beggin' her to live out there, instead of in this nice little house, here, that her mother left her. Of course she wouldn't—no sense in livin' on Sixpenny, and nobody but a crazy fellow like Bill Tubbs would ever have thought of it."

"Fell off a tree?" exclaimed Djuna. "How did that happen?"

"Oh, I don't know," said Mr. Truelove. "I wasn't here at the time. That was twenty years ago. Pickin' cherries, maybe, or apples. You'll have to ask some of the old folks around here, if you want to know. Old Cap'n Atterbury—he'd know the whole story, if you want to hear it, probably. He's known Aunt Patty ever since she was born. Knew her father, and her grandfather, too, I reckon. He'll tell you plenty o' stories about them."

"Mr. Truelove, what will Aunt Patty do, if they can't get the *Patagonia* off the rocks?" asked Djuna anxiously. "How can she go out to get the lobsters from her lobster pots?"

"Well, now, that's a question," said Mr. Truelove, gloomily. "If she can't save the *Patagonia*, or get herself another boat, she's bound to have a worse time than ever. That's about all she's got to depend on, lobsterin', and summer boarders like you."

"How much would a new boat cost, Mr. Truelove?" asked Djuna.

"Well, it would cost plenty," said Mr. Truelove. "I reckon you couldn't get one the size of the *Patagonia* for less than a thousand dollars. What's the use of talkin'? She hain't got the money, anyway."

"A thousand dollars!" exclaimed Djuna, horrified. "Why, that's an awful lot of money! And you said she hasn't got any money at all!"

"Not unless she's got something saved up that nobody

knows about," said Mr. Truelove. "As far as I know, she'll either have to sell her house, or starve. It's terrible!"

Djuna's heart sank. He walked home to Aunt Patty's house very slowly, trying to think what he could possibly do to help her.

Aunt Patty was feeling so badly that she went upstairs to her bedroom and lay down, a little while after Djuna got home. So Djuna decided to go back to Billy's house and talk things over with him.

"I asked Mr. Truelove if he saw anybody sneaking around the *Patagonia* last night," said Djuna, "and he said he didn't see anybody at all. He didn't see anybody last night, he said, except Harvey Bohnett and his brother."

"Harvey and Bonehead?" exclaimed Billy. "Gee, they're so mean they would do anything! I'll bet they did it! I'll bet they stole it just on purpose to wreck it! I'm going to tell my father! They ought to be arrested, right away!"

"Well, I don't know," said Djuna. "Mr. Truelove said he saw them go away, and the *Patagonia* was still there, after they left. I guess you couldn't arrest them if nobody saw them take it. Mr. Truelove didn't even hear anybody, all night long, so he thinks the rope just got untied, all by itself, and the *Patagonia* just floated off."

"He's crazy!" exclaimed Billy indignantly. "She couldn't have got all the way out there, unless somebody towed her there! Who does he think lit that lantern, anyway? Does he think that got lit all by itself? Didn't you tell him about that?"

"No," said Djuna, "I didn't say anything about it. What was the use? He was asleep, of course, when it happened. He doesn't know anything about it, that's all."

"I wouldn't be too sure about that," said Billy, scowling. "Maybe he knows all about it. Anyway, I think we ought to see if we can find out about Harvey and Bonehead from somebody else, if we can. I know where they are now. They're over at the Harbor House. Come on, let's go over there and see."

"Well, all right," said Djuna, "but it's no use asking *them*. Do you know anybody else there, somebody who might know where they were last night?"

"Sure, I know Mr. Primrose," said Billy. "He's the colored man that takes care of the rooms. We can ask *him*."

When they got to the Harbor House, they could see the Bohnett brothers and two or three other men sitting on the front porch, but Billy led the way around to the back door, where they found Mr. Primrose resting on a bench in the back yard.

"Hello, Billy," he said, grinning, "you got that trick dog of yours with you? I can't see him, but I expect he ain't far behind you."

"I left him at home," said Billy. "We're G men."

"Oh, you is, is you?" said Mr. Primrose. "You ain't aimin' to arrest *me*, is you, Mister G Man Reckless?"

"Not if you tell us what we want to know," said Billy. "We just want to know if Harvey Bohnett and Bonehead were here last night. Were they?"

"They certainly was!" exclaimed Mr. Primrose. "And how! They come in just when I was fixin' to go to baid and kept me runnin' up and down stairs with ice water, and this and that, most all night long! Then they tell me be sure and wake 'em at seven o'clock, so I does. Seems like I hardly got any sleepin' done *at* all!"

Billy and Djuna looked at each other.

"That's just what Mr. Truelove said," whispered Djuna. "He said it was pretty late when they left his wharf. Then they must have come right over here. Oh, gee!"

"Anything else you gentlemen want to know?" said Mr. Primrose. "Because if there ain't, I aim to catch up on my sleep some more."

And he settled back on the bench and closed his eyes with a sigh. "Goo'bye!" he said.

Djuna and Billy went back to Billy's house feeling completely discouraged. If it was not the Bohnett brothers who had taken Aunt Patty's boat, who could it have been?

"The best thing we can do is to go and hunt around the wharf where the *Patagonia* was," said Djuna. "Maybe we can find some footprints, or something. Maybe we won't, but we can try, anyway."

And try they did, for all the rest of the morning, searching over every inch of the wharf where the *Patagonia* had been tied and all the beach near it; but they could find nothing at all that looked like a clue.

Djuna went home, got something to eat and then put on his bathing suit and hurried down to the Point. The wind had gone down, and the waves had almost flattened out. The tide was so low that the rocks were now out of water, and the poor old *Patagonia* was perched on top of the rocks on which she had been driven by the wind. Djuna waded out to her. The water was only knee-deep, now. When he reached the *Patagonia,* she was a sorry sight. The sharp points of the rocks had crushed holes in her planks, and the water that had rushed in was now dripping out again, so that it looked as if she were bleeding.

Just as he got there, Captain Reckless' motorboat came along from the harbor, towing a rowboat behind it, and Captain Reckless anchored in the channel as close as he could get to the *Patagonia.* He had brought Mr. Truelove and the old fisherman, Mr. Jackson, with him. They were all wearing boots. They got into the rowboat and came over to the *Patagonia,* bringing some new planks, hammers and saws, a bucket of tar, a bundle of tow and oakum, and other tools. The tide was now so low that they had to get out of the rowboat when they were still a little way from the *Patagonia,* so they waded the rest of the way in their boots, dragging the rowboat behind them. Billy had come with them, and splashed along in the lead.

Captain Reckless walked all around the *Patagonia,* looking her over very carefully to see how much damage had been done.

"Well," he said at last, "she's jammed in there so tight that there's no use trying to patch her up from outside. We'll have to see what we can do about plugging up those holes from the inside, enough to get her floated again."

He climbed on board the *Patagonia,* and Djuna scrambled up beside him. Captain Reckless opened up the hatch cover beside the little wheelhouse and peered in.

"Say, what's this?" he exclaimed. Djuna squeezed up beside him and ducked under his elbow to see.

The boards that had separated the wheelhouse from the rest of the forepeak space had been sawed through and ripped off! The broken boards and splinters of wood floated in the water in the bottom of the boat. Through the hole that had been made, they could see the inside of the wheelhouse.

"Just plain meanness!" said Captain Reckless angrily. "The skunks that took her weren't satisfied with just stealing the boat, they had to try to tear her to pieces, too!"

"Gee, what did they want to do *that* for?" exclaimed Djuna. "Were they trying to make her sink?"

"No, I just can't see any reason for it at all," said Captain Reckless, shaking his head in bewilderment. "You could tear out all that part and still it wouldn't let any water in. It just looks to me like plain crazy meanness. If I ever find out who did this, I'll make him wish he hadn't! Well, we can't waste time on that now. First thing to do is to get some of this water out of the bilge. No time to lose!"

Leaning over the side of the *Patagonia,* he asked Mr. Truelove and Mr. Jackson to hand the bilge pump up to him, and then to come and help him. The bilge pump was a long hollow tube, with a piston inside it which was moved up and down in the tube by a long rod with a handle at the top. When the bottom of the tube was put into the water which had leaked into the *Patagonia* and the handle was pushed up and down, the water was pumped up. It was very hard work, and the three men took turns at pumping. But when they had worked at it for about an hour, the water had been pumped out so that they could reach the broken planks near the *Patagonia's* keel.

Then they set to work with their tools and patched up the holes in the *Patagonia* with new planks, which they fastened very strongly to the old ones, and then they stuffed the oakum under the edges of the planks and smeared tar over it, so that no more water could leak in.

This was a long job, and although they worked as fast as they could, it was six o'clock by the time they had finished. The tide had reached its lowest point at three o'clock, and now it was creeping back in again, and the rowboat was floating again.

"There!" said Captain Reckless, as they finished the work. "In a couple of hours more, the tide will be high enough to float the *Patagonia* and we can pull her off."

"Hurrah!" yelled Billy and Djuna. They had been watching the whole job with breathless interest, and had even been able to help some, by handing tools to the men, when they asked for them.

"Let's go and tell Aunt Patty!" said Billy, starting to climb down from the *Patagonia's* deck.

Djuna looked around to see if he had forgotten anything, and suddenly remembered the lantern he had found in the wheelhouse that morning, and had put into the locker. He ran back and got it, and showed it to Captain Reckless.

"Will it be all right if I take this back to Aunt Patty's house?" he asked. "I don't think there's any oil left in it, because it was smoking so when I found it."

"Sure, take it along," said Captain Reckless. "And if you can figure out who lit that lantern last night, I'll give you a dollar! It would be worth that much just to get my hands on the cowardly pup!"

"Gee, I don't see how we can ever find out!" said Djuna. He hesitated. Staring at the lantern as if it were something he had never seen before in all his life, a strange look suddenly spread over his face. He drew a deep breath.

"Don't tell anybody I took this lantern, will you?" he whispered.

"Why, no, I won't say anything about it," said Captain Reckless, surprised. "Say, you don't think you know who it was, do you?"

Djuna shook his head, and began to look embarrassed. "No," he said, "I just thought—well, anyway, I was just thinking!"

Captain Reckless chuckled. "You sound like Billy," he said.

"Yes, sir," said Djuna. And he hurried over the side of the *Patagonia*, to get away before he was asked any more questions that he couldn't answer.

But Billy was waiting for him, and, of course, saw the lantern as soon as Djuna caught up to him.

"Where'd you get the lantern?" he asked. "What are you going to do with it?"

"Oh, nothing," said Djuna. "It was the one in the wheel-house. I'm just going to take it to Aunt Patty. Say, do you know what I think?"

"No, what?" asked Billy.

"Well, I was just thinking about burglars," said Djuna. "Burglars and the *Patagonia*."

"I don't know what you're talking about," said Billy. "You mean it was a burglar that stole the *Patagonia*?"

"No, that's not what I mean," said Djuna. "I mean, suppose a burglar steals a pocketbook out of a house. Do you suppose he *keeps* that pocketbook?"

"Why, I don't know," said Billy. "Doesn't he?"

"Of course not!" said Djuna. "He takes the money out of it and then he throws the pocketbook away! Now do you see?"

"No," said Billy, looking more puzzled than ever.

"Well, that's what the man did when he took the

Patagonia, don't you see?" insisted Djuna. "He didn't want the boat—he wanted something that was *in* it! You see? So after he had had a chance to hunt for whatever it was he wanted, he threw the boat away! Just like an empty pocketbook, see?"

"For Pete's sake!" exclaimed Billy excitedly. "Of course!"

"The only thing is," Djuna went on, still thinking hard, "nobody can tell whether he got what he was looking for, or not. Maybe he found it, and maybe he didn't. We've got to ask Aunt Patty. Gee, I hope she didn't have anything hidden in there, that was worth a lot of money!"

"So do I," said Billy. "But, gee, not even a G man could ever catch whoever it was that took the *Patagonia!* He's gone, and there's a million places he might have gone to. He was in a boat, of course. He might have gone anywhere, so where would you look? Boats don't leave any tracks on the water. No tracks that last, anyway."

"No," agreed Djuna, "they don't. But a boat like the *Patagonia* is worth a lot of money. Mr. Truelove said it would cost a thousand dollars to get one like it! I don't think we need to find any tracks."

Billy stared at him. "What do you mean?" he demanded.

"Well, look," said Djuna, eagerly. "Do you suppose a man that stole a boat worth a thousand dollars would throw it away, if he had a chance to keep it? Of course he wouldn't! The only reason he let the *Patagonia* go, and let her get blown onto the rocks, was because *he didn't dare bring her back!*"

Billy's eyes opened wide, because Djuna's voice was so excited. But he still didn't see what Djuna meant.

"Well, of course, he wouldn't dare to bring her back,

if he had stolen her," he said. "He would get caught right away."

"That's just what I mean!" cried Djuna. "He could take her anywhere else, a long way from here, and sell her, or use her, and nobody there would know where he got her from. But if he lived here in Stony Harbor, where everybody knew him, and knew Aunt Patty, then, of course, he couldn't bring the *Patagonia* back here!"

"Oh!" said Billy. "I see now! If he *wasn't* somebody that lives in Stony Harbor, he could have kept right on going, and could take the *Patagonia* wherever he went! But he knew he *had* to come back here, and so he *had* to leave her out in the middle of the Sound!"

"That's the way it was, I should think," said Djuna, looking very serious. "So we'd better be careful. Whoever did it is probably right here in Stony Harbor right now, this very minute. You can't tell who it might be. Don't you say a word to *anybody*, Billy, because it might be the very one!"

Billy looked quickly around, in a worried sort of way, but the only thing he saw was old Mr. Jackson's cow, trying to find some grass in the stony field next to the stone lighthouse.

"No, I'll be careful," he whispered. "But, gee, who do you suppose it is?"

"Well, I thought at first it might be that old Harvey Bohnett and his brother," said Djuna. "But now that we've found out that they were at the Harbor House all night, I don't know at all."

"Then what shall we do next?" asked Billy.

"We've got to ask Aunt Patty what was in her boat," said Djuna. "That's the first thing to find out."

They hurried on to Aunt Patty's and into her kitchen.

"It's fixed, Aunt Patty!" they yelled. "Your boat's fixed! Hurrah!"

Aunt Patty was so glad that she almost cried.

"I've been so worried I didn't know what to do," she said, wiping the tears of joy from her eyes. "I couldn't even bear to go down to the Point and look at the *Patagonia*, I was so afraid she couldn't be saved. Have they really got her afloat?"

"Well, they're just waiting for the tide," said Djuna. "They've fixed up the leaks, and as soon as she floats, Captain Reckless is going to pull her around to his wharf, so he can fix her some more."

"Oh, thank goodness!" exclaimed Aunt Patty. "Now, you boys sit down and have your dinner. I expect you're pretty hungry, after all you've done today. I declare, I'm so thankful I'm as hungry as a bear!"

They all sat down at the table and while Aunt Patty heaped their plates, Djuna told her about the strange way in which a hole had been chopped through the side of the *Patagonia's* wheelhouse, by the person who had stolen her boat.

"What were they looking for, Aunt Patty?" he asked. "You didn't keep any money, or anything special, in there, did you?"

"Money?" repeated Aunt Patty. "I haven't got any money, child. And if I had, I wouldn't have kept it in any such place as that. That's certainly queer, their ripping out those boards, just out of meanness. I can't imagine why they should want to do it!"

"Didn't you *ever* keep anything in there?" persisted Djuna.

"No, not as far as I can remember," said Aunt Patty slowly. "No, I'm sure I never did." Then she smiled. "But that reminds me," she went on. "There was a little cubbyhole between the wall of the wheelhouse and the hatchway partition. Captain Tubbs, that was my husband, used to keep things in there. But that was so long ago I'd almost forgotten."

"What did he keep in there?" exclaimed Djuna eagerly, looking at Billy.

"Oh, just all sorts of odds and ends, anything he happened to tuck away," said Aunt Patty. "Fish hooks, and lines, and his pipe and tobacco, and this, that, and the other thing. I used to laugh at it, it was such a regular squirrel's nest, so he got to calling it his squirrel's nest. But after—well, after he was gone—I cleaned it out and boarded up the wall, so as to make more room in the hold. I'd forgotten all about it, till just now."

"And didn't he ever keep any money in there?" asked Djuna, disappointedly.

"Mercy, no!" said Aunt Patty. "If he had, I would have found it."

7. Patagonia

THE *Patagonia* floated off the rocks at high tide that evening, and the temporary patches that Captain Reckless had put in her kept her from leaking too much while he towed her back to the harbor, at the end of a long rope. He told Aunt Patty that he would have to rip off the old planks and put on new planking, which would take him two or three weeks. In order to do this work, he had to haul the *Patagonia* up out of the water, on the sloping beach by his house, and prop her up with big logs. Billy and Djuna spent hours in watching him do it, and sometimes Captain Reckless would let them help a little.

But Djuna never stopped thinking about the mysterious way in which the *Patagonia* had been stolen and set adrift, and the mysterious way in which Aunt Patty's darning egg and the umbrella top that looked like an egg had disappeared from her house. More and more he thought about what Mr. Truelove had said to him, about the way Aunt Patty's troubles had begun when she was a little girl, when her father died and didn't leave any money for her mother and Patty to live on. He remembered that Mr. Truelove had told him that old Captain Atterbury knew Aunt Patty's father and mother, before they died.

At last he decided that he would ask Captain Atterbury about them.

Captain Atterbury's little house was on the east side of the village, with a front porch that looked out over the water. Captain Atterbury was sitting on the porch when Djuna got there. He was very short and very fat, with a red face and white hair, and bushy white eyebrows. He took the pipe out of his mouth and stared at Djuna as he came up the front walk.

"Well, young man, what can I do for you?" he asked. His voice rumbled.

"My name's Djuna," said Djuna, bashfully. "I'm staying at Aunt Patty Tubbs' house this summer. Could I ask you something, please, Captain Atterbury?"

"Oh, I heard Aunt Patty had a boy boardin' with her

this summer," rumbled the Captain. "So you're the one, hey? Come aboard, come aboard, and set down. What is it ye want to know? Fire away, and ask all the questions ye want."

Djuna sat down in the chair the Captain pointed to, and squirmed around in it. He didn't know exactly how to begin.

"Well," he said, "could you tell me why Aunt Patty's boat is named the *Patagonia?*"

Captain Atterbury stared, chuckled, coughed and wheezed. "That's a funny one!" he chuckled. "Aunt Patty wouldn't tell you herself, would she? No, of course not! She's awful closemouthed, when it comes to anything that has to do with Bill Tubbs. Well, *I* can tell ye, but the whole story goes back a mighty long way. About a hundred and fifty years, as a matter of fact. But just don't ye hurry me, and I'll tell it to ye."

He refilled his pipe, lighted it, and puffed away at it, his eyes twinkling.

"Yes, sir, the answer to that question of yours goes 'way back to the year George Washington was 'lected President," he said. "Because that was the year when Aunt Patty's great-grandfather, Ben Greene, was fust made captain of a whaling ship. A little ship named the *Osprey*, she was."

"Oh, Aunt Patty told me about him!" exclaimed Djuna. "She's got an old wooden sea chest up in her attic, with his initials on it! I saw it!"

Captain Atterbury nodded. "That's the man," he said. "We'll come to that sea chest, later. As I was sayin', Cap'n Ben Greene was a mighty young man when he took command of the *Osprey*, but he'd been at sea ever since he was a boy, and he was a right smart officer. That fust voyage of his, he sailed northward, huntin' black whales, where he'd been before. He was gone a year, and came back with full barrels, sold 'em, and started off again. This time, he sailed south, after sperm whale. He had pretty good luck that voyage and the next; and after the second one he got married. Then he set sail on his third voyage south, and that one turned out even better than the others. But he was mighty lucky that he got back at all, from that one."

"What happened?" exclaimed Djuna.

"Well, that voyage, he sailed even farther south than he had before," said Captain Atterbury. "He'd heard tales that the English whalers, and some of our men from Nantucket, too, were findin' plenty of whale down around the Falkland Islands, so he kept right on a-goin'. He had close to ten thousand miles o' sailin' to do, before he got there, and it must have taken that little ship o' his all of three months, if not more. It took 'em another three months of cruisin' around the whaling grounds before they had struck enough whales to fill their barrels, and start for home. Their food and water was gettin' low, so they put in at the Falkland Islands, to try to get some. But the Falklands are a barren place, and the men at the tradin' post there couldn't spare them what they wanted. So Cap'n Greene decided he'd steer a course for the nearest part of South America, and see if he could get any supplies from the Indians on the coast.

"That coast was only a matter of three hundred miles west of the Falklands, so he came in sight of it in less than a week, although the wind was contrary and drove 'em a good deal south of their course. They landed on the coast of Tierra del Fuego.

"It was a terrible cold windy country, with the mountains off in the distance all covered with snow, but there was plenty of streams running through the valleys, and they filled all their water kegs with fresh water. They found an Indian village on the bank of one of the creeks, and tried to make the Indians understand that they wanted to get corn and fresh meat, but the Indians didn't have any.

"They sailed on toward the north and pretty soon they came to the coast of Patagonia, where there were no more mountains in sight, just low treeless plains. There were wide gravelly beaches between the sea and the low cliffs where the plains began, and on some of these beaches there were herds of sea lions, thousands and thousands of 'em, barking and bellowing and makin' the most awful noise.

"They knew the sea lions weren't fit to eat, but they kept on sailing close to the coast, hoping to see another Indian village, but there weren't any. Finally they came to a river, and sailed up it a little way, and anchored. Cap'n Greene and four or five men in his crew got into a boat and rowed ashore, with their muskets, to see if they could find any game.

"When they had climbed up the sand banks by the beach, they saw a whole herd of funny-lookin' animals out on the plains, a little way off. They looked sort of like deer, and sort of like camels, but they had long woolly hair. Cap'n Greene found out afterwards they were what are called huanacos. He and his men crept around on their knees, behind bushes, until they got up close to them, and then they all fired, all at once, and killed two of the huanacos, and the rest of 'em galloped away like mad. They dragged the two that they had shot back to their boat, and Cap'n Greene told his men to take them out to the ship and then come back for him, while he waited to see if he could find anything else to shoot.

"He wandered back on the plains by himself, and all of a sudden he saw a band of about a dozen Indians galloping toward him on their ponies. He ran toward the beach as fast as he could, but they caught up with him and surrounded him. He pointed his gun at the one who seemed to be the chief, and pulled the trigger, but it missed fire. Before he could fix it, two or three of the Indians jumped down and grabbed him, and the rest crowded all around him.

"They were all big powerful fellows, dirty and greasy, and so ugly lookin' that he thought they were goin' to kill him, sure. They jerked his gun out of his hands, and all of them began jabbering away at him. They kept sayin' somethin' that sounded like 'Run! Run!' but he couldn't figure out how they expected him to run, as long as they kept holdin' on to him by both his arms. But finally some of them began makin' signs, pointin' at the ship, and makin' believe they was drinkin' out of a bottle, and he begin to understand that what they was sayin' was *'Ron! Ron!'* which was the furrin word that meant rum. So he nodded, and tried to make them understand he'd get it for them if they'd let him go, but they shook their heads and jabbered worse than ever.

"But at last he got the chief to understand that all of the Indians except the two who were guarding him must lie down on the ground, so that the men in the boat couldn't see them, and be afraid to land. The chief told the two Indians to take him nearer the beach, but not to let go of him.

"But when they got within a few feet of the edge of the sandbank overlooking the beach, Cap'n Greene suddenly threw himself against one of the two Indians and tripped him up, so that all three of them fell in a heap and they all rolled over and over down the bank. In the scramble, the Indians let go. The minute they struck the bottom, Cap'n Greene picked himself up and ran as hard as he could go, toward the boat. The boat was still fifty feet from shore, but he jumped into the water and began to swim for it. The water was ice cold, and his clothes almost dragged him down, but he managed to keep up until the boat reached him, and he was pulled in. The Indians ran for their lives.

"That was the last time they tried to land on the coast of Patagonia. They kept right on for another thousand miles, without seein' a single town on the coast, until they came to a big Portygee city named Montevideo. They got all the fresh provisions they needed there, and came on home. Cap'n Greene sold that cargo of whale oil for so much money that he sold the *Osprey* and bought a bigger ship. He was so thankful for escapin' from those Indians in Patagonia, that he named his new ship the *Patagonia*."

"Gee, that was exciting!" Djuna exclaimed. "Is that why Aunt Patty calls her boat the *Patagonia*?"

"Now, wait, that's not all the story," said Captain Atterbury. "That's just the beginnin'. About three or four years after that, Cap'n Greene's wife had a baby boy. If you want to know the year he was born, I can tell ye—it was the same year President Washington died. Well, the baby was named Hiram, and it wasn't but three years after he was born that Cap'n Greene got swept off the deck of the *Patagonia* in a storm and got drownded. The fust mate brought the ship home, and Cap'n Greene's sea chest with it, and that's the same old chest you saw in Aunt Patty's attic. Aunt Patty may have told ye, I was up there the other day, tryin' to find his log books. You didn't come across any of 'em, did ye, bub?"

"No, sir," said Djuna. "I wish I had! What did they do with Captain Greene's ship after the mate brought it back?"

"Well, Cap'n Greene's widow, she had to sell her, of course," said Captain Atterbury, lighting his pipe again. "She had her boy Hiram to bring up, and she did. She kept him at school till he was sixteen, and then he went to sea, just like his father. He was a mighty able young man, and by the time he was twenty he was picked for mate on a right stout little sloop that went all the way from Stony Harbor, away south of Patagonia on a voyage for fur seals, and discovered land closer to the South Pole than anybody else ever had. Next voyage, he was mate on a sealer that sailed around Cape Horn and went away up to the Aleutian Islands, huntin' seals. When they had got their hold full o' sealskins, they went on acrosst the Pacific and sold them in Canton, Chiny. And Hiram, young as he was, made a right smart lot o' money as his share o' what they got for the sealskins, and the tea and the Chiny goods they brought back with 'em. Well, he kept on makin' more voyages to Chiny, and he saved his money, and it wa'n't long before he was made cap'n of a ship that was built and owned right here in Stony Harbor. But Cap'n Hiram Greene didn't get married till he was nigh on to fifty years old. By that time he had saved up a mint o' money, and he built a ship of his own, and named her the *Patagonia,* same as his father's was named. And the day after she was launched, blessed if his wife didn't bring him a baby boy! What with his new ship and his new son, I reckon Cap'n Hiram Greene was jest about as proud a man as ever walked the streets o' Stony Harbor.

"But he kept on makin' voyages. That was the year gold was discovered in Californy, and the whole country went crazy over the news. Men was payin' high to get out there, and Cap'n Greene made money hand over fist, takin' 'em from New York out to San Francisco, around Cape Horn. The *Patagonia* was a fast sailin' ship, though she wa'n't a full clipper, and she went back and forth from New York to Californy as regular as a ferry-boat. In the next ten years, she made a dozen or more voyages to San Francisco and back, with a couple o' voyages to Chiny thrown in. And then she ran into a typhoon in the Chiny Sea, and was lost, with all hands. And if you want to know what year that was, I can tell ye—it was the year Lincoln was fust elected President.

"Well, there was the Cap'n's wife left a widow, with her little boy—Amos, his name was—but the Cap'n had left her plenty o' money. She was rich. She kept on livin' in New York, where she had been livin' while the Cap'n was makin' his voyages to Californy, and she lived in style. She mighty near spoiled that boy of hers, Amos, givin' him everything he asked for. She gave him a pony, and the boy got throwed off it and broke his leg, and he was always lame after that, all the rest of his life. Bein' lame maybe was one reason why he never went to sea, like his father and grandfather, but his mother was set against it, anyway, for fear he get drownded like they was. But she brought him up like a young prince, or something, and after she died, and he come into the money, he went on livin' like a prince. He didn't get married till after he was forty—married a girl named Hatch, rich Boston folks. But it wa'n't no time at all till he had spent what money he had left, and whatever money his wife brought him, and he brought her back here to live, in that same little house Aunt Patty lives in now, because that was mighty near all he had left. It was his own fault, for he'd throwed away his money like water, all his life, and he said so himself. He took pride in it, seemed like.

"He was a great hand at talkin', used to talk by the hour, if he could find anybody to listen to him. I was a young feller then, and I liked to listen to him. It was him that told me what I've just been tellin' ye about his father and grandfather. I used to go over to see him, winter nights when I had nothin' else to do, and listen to his yarns.

"I remember him settin' there, in his chair by the fire-place, and bangin' on the hearthstones with his cane—he always had his cane with him, account of his lame leg, never let go of it, day or night—I'd give a mint o' money for that cane—and he always would end up by grinnin' and sayin', 'My dad had money, and my grand-dad had money, and now look at me—not a thing left of all they had, except this!' And then he'd laugh and say, 'But someday my ship will come in, one of these days, and when she does, I'll name her *Patagonia,* just for luck!'

"Of course his luck never got any better, but when his baby girl was born, he was as excited as if he had come into a million dollars. 'She's my luck!' he says. 'She's better than a ship!'

"And, bless my soul, do ye know what he did? He called that baby Patagonia!"

Djuna's eyes opened wide. "You mean that's Aunt Patty?" he exclaimed.

"That's who it was," said Captain Atterbury. "And a cuter baby you never saw!"

"But didn't he have a ship at all?" asked Djuna. "What was the ship he was looking for, the ship that was going to come in?"

Captain Atterbury laughed. "Don't you know what that means, bub?" he asked. "That's not a real ship—that's just somethin' you say when you're hopin' that a lot of money will come to you, unexpected. No, Amos Greene didn't have a ship, and never did. He was just as poor as a church mouse when he died. He didn't own even so much as a rowboat."

"He didn't?" said Djuna, looking puzzled. "Then where did Aunt Patty get her boat? Where did she get the *Patagonia?*"

"I'm comin' to that," said Captain Atterbury. "You asked me why she named it the *Patagonia,* didn't ye? The answer to that is, she didn't. It wa'n't her boat, to begin with, and she didn't have the namin' of it. 'Tain't likely she'd give it her own name anyway. No, sir, it wa'n't her that named it the *Patagonia.*"

"Well, who did?" persisted Djuna.

"That good-for-nothin' Bill Tubbs!" said Captain Atterbury, flushing angrily. "The fellow she married, after her mother died! That was the way he got on the soft side of her—he figured it would please her if he named his boat after her, and it did. He was always hangin' around her, and finally she married him. Maybe she had some sort of notion that her luck would turn, if she had a boat named the *Patagonia*, just like her granddaddy and her great-granddaddy. But it didn't. The luckiest thing that ever happened to her was when Bill Tubbs fell off'n the tree and broke his wuthless neck!"

Captain Atterbury had spoken so angrily that Djuna was surprised. "Didn't she like him?" he asked. "Was he mean to Aunt Patty, or something?"

"He never give her a minute's peace," said Captain Atterbury. "He was always pesterin' her to sell that little house o' hers, just so he could git his hands on the money, and wouldn't have to work. Wanted her to sell the house and go live in that little shack of his on Sixpenny Island, where nobody in his right mind would ever want to live. But Bill Tubbs was *never* in his right mind, from the time he was born. Crazy as a June bug, that's *my* opinion."

"Did he really act crazy?" asked Djuna, wonderingly. "Aunt Patty wouldn't have married him if he'd been crazy, would she?"

Captain Atterbury snorted. "Bird nestin'!" he exclaimed scornfully. "Huntin' birds eggs! A grown-up man actin' like a boy! If that ain't crazy, what is?"

Djuna almost jumped out of his chair. "Gee, that's funny!" he exclaimed. "Aunt Patty—" And then he stopped short.

"Yessir, he wasted enough time huntin' birds' nests to have made hisself rich, if it had been any sensible sort o' work," Captain Atterbury went on indignantly, without noticing Djuna's interruption. "And it ended up by his fallin' out o' that tree, just like he might have expected!"

Djuna looked puzzled. "Why?" he asked. "Why did he expect to fall out of it?"

"Because he should have known better, that's why," said Captain Atterbury impatiently. "Anybody had ought to know better than to try to get eggs out o' an eagle's nest! No doubt about it—that old eagle must have flew at him so hard he knocked him right off!"

"An eagle?" exclaimed Djuna, excitedly. "Gee, we saw an eagle. Billy Reckless and I saw one, out on Eagle Rock! A great big one, all dark brown, except his head was all white! Gee, he looked awful fierce! Was that the kind that had the nest?"

"So you saw one, did ye?" asked Captain Atterbury, looking surprised. "That's the fust one I've heard tell of, around here, for a mighty long while! And 'twas flyin' around Eagle Rock, ye say? Out there to Haypenny Island?"

"Yes, sir," said Djuna, "we sailed out there, in Billy's boat. And it lit right on the rock!"

Suddenly Djuna remembered something. "Golly!" he said. "When I told Aunt Patty about it, she looked awful funny! She almost cried! Gee, I guess it must have made her think about Mister Tubbs, the way the eagle killed him! I wish I hadn't said anything about it at all, but *I* didn't know."

"Of course you didn't know, bub," said Captain Atterbury comfortingly. "But that was right where it happened, right there at Eagle Rock."

"At Eagle Rock?" exclaimed Djuna in surprise. "But how could it? There *isn't* any tree at Eagle Rock!"

"Well, there was then," insisted Captain Atterbury. "Biggest pine tree you ever saw, a good hundred feet high. The eagles' nest was right at the top of it. Tree grew right out of a crack in the rock."

"But what became of it?" asked Djuna. "*We* didn't see any tree there."

"That tree blew down in the hurricane, twenty year ago," said Captain Atterbury. "Not enough anchorage for its roots. Kind o' like Aunt Patty's luck, we might say."

He looked at his watch and got to his feet. "Time I was givin' Missus Atterbury her medicine," he said. "You run along, bub, and come over again, any time ye're a mind to. Tell Aunt Patty the doctor says Missus Atterbury is comin' along real nice."

8. The Discouraged Detectives

AUNT PATTY was in the middle of housecleaning when Djuna got home, and had just finished sweeping the upstairs rooms.

"My goodness, it's about time I cleaned out that fireplace," she exclaimed, as she glanced around the front room. "I've been meaning to take those wood ashes out for a long time, but I never got around to it. Djuna, would you mind taking them out and dumping them on that strip of ground by the fence? I'm going to spade that up and plant some more flowers there, one of these days, and there's nothing better than wood ashes to mix in the ground, to make them grow."

Djuna got a dustpan and an old bucket and carried them out, and then swept out the fireplace carefully, till the hearth was clean. The fireplace was built of red bricks, and looked very neat. But Djuna stared at it in a puzzled sort of way.

"Where is the other fireplace, Aunt Patty?" he asked. "The one with the hearthstone?"

Aunt Patty looked startled. "Why, that's the only one!" she exclaimed. "What do you mean, child?"

"Well, Captain Atterbury said there was one with a hearthstone," said Djuna. "He said there was."

"Oh!" said Aunt Patty. "Well, that's so, there *was* one there, once. But that was years and years ago. I know what Captain Atterbury was thinking of. But *that* stone is over on Sixpenny Island, now. Captain Tubbs took it over there. He wanted it for a doorstep, and I told him he could have it if he would build a brick one for me. I always wanted a brick fireplace, anyway. Everybody else has stone ones, around here."

"Captain Atterbury told me a lot of things," said Djuna. "I think he's awful nice. Oh, I forgot—he said to tell you the doctor said Mrs. Atterbury is much better."

"Well, now, I'm glad to hear it!" exclaimed Aunt Patty, beaming. "That poor woman hadn't been one bit well, lately. Run along now, Djuna, if you want to—I've got some sewing to do, as soon as I finish cleaning."

Djuna hesitated. Then he asked the question that had come into his mind when Captain Atterbury had told him how Captain Tubbs, Aunt Patty's husband, had liked to collect birds' eggs.

"Aunt Patty," he said, "have you still got the birds' eggs Captain Tubbs got?"

Aunt Patty looked startled. "Why, no!" she said. "He never kept any of 'em—he sold 'em to Doctor Holder, as fast as he got 'em."

"Does he live here?" asked Djuna.

"Why, yes," said Aunt Patty. "He's the only doctor there is in this town. But he's pretty old, now. He knew my mother and father before I was born. Of course, he was just a young man, then. Mother never had any children except me, and she always wanted a boy. So Doctor Holder was just like a son to them. *They* thought a heap of him."

"Don't *you* like him?" asked Djuna.

"I've got nothing against Doctor Holder," said Aunt Patty, grimly. "He never liked my marrying Captain Tubbs, and neither did Captain Atterbury. But that's all over and done with. I don't hold it against either of 'em. Live and let live, that's *my* motto."

"Has Doctor Holder got all kinds of birds' eggs?" asked Djuna, wonderingly.

"Why, I suppose so," said Aunt Patty, beginning to sweep the room. "He used to."

"Gee, I'd like to see them," said Djuna. "Do you think he would show them to me?"

"I don't know why not," said Aunt Patty. "Why don't you ask him? Take Billy along with you—he'll show you where Doctor Holder lives."

Djuna called Champ and they set off together for Billy's house. They found Billy in his front yard. He was walking around and around in a circle on the grass, and every few feet he would yell, "Oops!" He was so busy doing this, he didn't notice them until they got right up to him.

"What are you doing?" asked Djuna.

Billy turned around, startled. "Oh, hello," he said. "I'm teaching Alberto how to jump through a hoop."

"What for?" asked Djuna.

"Well, I thought maybe I could sell him to the circus," said Billy. "If there was a circus came here, I'll bet I could sell him."

"*I* wouldn't sell him," said Djuna. "Not if he was *my* dog. But I'll bet you could get a lot of money for him. Say, listen, do you know where Doctor Holder lives?"

"Sure," said Billy. "Why?"

"Aunt Patty says he collects birds' eggs," said Djuna. "I thought maybe he'd let us look at them. Do you want to go over with me and ask him?"

"Sure," said Billy. "But I'm not going to take Alberto. He's all tired out. I guess I made him jump through the hoops a million times, I guess. Well, maybe not quite a million, but almost."

Billy led the way across the village till they came to Doctor Holder's house, and they rang the bell at the front door. Pretty soon Doctor Holder came to the door.

He was the oldest looking man Djuna had ever seen. He was tall and thin, his face was brown and wrinkled, and although he had no hair on top of his head, the hair at the back of his head was snow-white, and so long that it came down to his coat collar. But he smiled down at the boys and in a very kind voice asked them what they wanted.

"Could we please see your egg collection?" asked Billy.

"Come in, come in," said the old gentleman, opening the door wider. "I'll be glad to show it to you. I haven't looked at them, myself, for years, but I guess they're all here, still."

He led the way across the hall into his office, a high-ceilinged room cluttered up with old furniture. Tall mahogany cabinets, with glass doors, stood against the wall, their shelves crowded with bottles of all sorts of medicine. His desk, an old-fashioned roll-topped desk of dark walnut, was heaped with letters and papers; and every pigeonhole was stuffed with papers. Bookcases, their shelves filled with hundreds of books, stood on each side of the fireplace; and near them was an old, but comfortable-looking, deep armchair, its leather much worn and tattered. In one corner stood a pile of flat wooden boxes; and the old man, shuffling over to them on his slippered feet, began to lift these boxes one by one and carry them over to a table by the window. The boys hurried forward to help him, but the old doctor motioned them to wait.

"I'd better do this myself," he said. "I've never let anyone else touch them, some of these shells are so delicate that a touch might crush them. If I break one myself, then nobody else is to blame."

A pane of glass, which had become coated thick with dust since the last time it had been touched, served as a lid for the first of the big flat boxes which Doctor Holder brought to the table. He lifted it off and propped it up against the wall.

"Now, let's see what we have here," he said, as the boys came to the table to peer into the open box.

Inside, the box was divided by thin strips of wood into

twenty-four neat compartments, each one filled with soft cotton batting. Gently removing the cotton, Doctor Holder displayed the treasured eggs, while the boys exclaimed in admiration of them.

The robin, the song sparrow, the wood thrush, the woodpecker, the seagull—the eggs of each of these, and of a hundred other kinds of birds were cradled there in the boxes.

The first of the three boxes that Doctor Holder brought out contained the eggs of the smallest birds, such as sparrows and warblers. The second box held the eggs of medium-sized birds. The eggs in the third box were so big that there was room in the box for only nine of them.

"These are mostly eggs of different kinds of hawks," said Doctor Holder. "This one, this pale bluish white one, is a marsh hawk's egg. I happened to find the nest one day when I was out hunting. It was just a heap of twigs right on a dry spot of ground, in among the swamp grass. There were five eggs in the nest, but I took only this one.

"This next one, the big white one with the brown spots, is a hen hawk's egg. The nest was at the top of a big pine tree. The farmer who brought it to me took all three eggs from the nest. He said he didn't want any more hawks killing his chickens.

"And this white egg, the biggest one, is an eagle's egg."

Both boys looked at it excitedly. "An eagle's egg!" they exclaimed in one breath.

Doctor Holder nodded his head sadly. "Yes," he said, "and that egg cost a man his life."

Djuna looked surprised. "But how did he get it?" he

exclaimed. "Do you mean that's the one that Mister Tubbs tried to get?"

Doctor Holder glanced at him sharply. "Oh, then you've heard that story, have you?" he asked. "Who told you about it?"

"Yes, sir, Captain Atterbury told me," said Djuna. "But he said the eagles fought Mister Tubbs when he climbed up to the nest and made him fall off before he got the eggs."

"That's only partly right," said Doctor Holder. "I was the first one to climb up to the nest, not Billy Tubbs. I was lucky enough to climb up there when both the birds were away. There were two eggs in the nest. I took this one, and came down safe. But I told Billy Tubbs, afterwards, that I had left one egg in the nest, and I'm sorry I did. He tried to get it, and he fell. Don't you boys ever try a thing like that, it's too dangerous. It's a good thing that the eagles don't nest in this neighborhood any more."

"But we saw one!" cried both boys at once.

"What's that?" said Doctor Holder. "Are you sure? Sure it wasn't a hawk?"

"It was, too, an eagle!" exclaimed Billy hotly. "We saw it right up close!"

And both boys proceeded to tell the old gentleman just how they had seen the great bird flying over Haypenny Island and how it had perched on Eagle Rock, only a few feet away from them. Doctor Holder listened attentively, nodding his head as they described the bird, and when they had finished he agreed that it was certainly an eagle.

"Well, that was a bald eagle, and no mistake," he said.

"But that doesn't mean that it has a nest anywhere near here. It may have flown from hundreds of miles away. It's a rare sight, here. You boys have seen something that few others have seen, nowadays."

He was about to put the glass lid back on the wooden tray holding the eggs, when Djuna asked him to wait.

"What kind of an egg is this one?" he asked, pointing at the largest of all the big eggs in the box. "Is that an ostrich egg, Doctor Holder?"

The old gentleman smiled. "Oh, no," he said. "That's nowhere near as big as an ostrich egg. If I had one, you'd see the difference. But it's a very interesting specimen. That egg has traveled the whole way around the world. Aunt Patty's father gave it to me. And he told me that his father brought it home from one of his long voyages, as a present for him, when he was a small boy. I imagine it must be almost a hundred years old. It's really quite wonderful that it was never broken, in all these years."

The boys stared at it. It was really a huge egg, almost three inches long. Its color was light brownish, like some hens' eggs, but it had blotches of grayish and pale purple color here and there, and spots of light reddish brown, also. It was almost as thick as it was long.

"What kind of an egg is it?" repeated Djuna wonderingly.

Doctor Holder rubbed his bald head. "I really can't remember," he said slowly. "I'm sure Amos Greene must have told me, when he gave it to me, but that's so long ago that I can't remember. Dear me, this is really annoying!"

"Where did it come from?" asked Billy.

"Well, that I can't be sure of, either," said the old man, as he put the glass lid back on the box. "Amos' father made very long voyages, you know. If I'm not mistaken, when he came home from that voyage he had sailed to China by way of Cape Horn and came back by way of the Cape of Good Hope. He might have stopped in Valparaiso, in Chile. There's a big bird called the condor in the high mountains down there. Perhaps he bought the egg there. He stopped at San Francisco, too, I'm sure. And from California he sailed on to China. But I just can't remember, for the life of me, where Captain Greene got that egg to bring home to his son. It might be a condor's egg, but I'm not sure. Well, well, I'll think of it, one of these days."

When he had put the boxes back in the corner and dusted off his hands, the boys thanked him for showing them the collection, and Doctor Holder invited them to come again whenever they liked. As they were going toward the front door, Djuna began to smile.

"What's so funny?" said Billy, noticing the smile.

"Oh, I just thought of a joke," said Djuna. "If that big egg came from China, then it's no wonder it never got broken, even if it is a hundred years old, because it's really a china egg."

"Oh, for Pete's sake!" said Billy, giggling. "That's the worst joke I ever heard."

"And if it was a china egg," Djuna went on stubbornly, "then you could use it for a nest egg."

Old Doctor Holder was just opening the door for them. He turned around and looked at Djuna in a very queer way.

"What's that?" he said sharply. "What nest egg are you talking about?"

The boys were surprised by the way he spoke. "Why, I don't know," said Djuna. "We weren't talking about a real one. We were just joking."

"Just joking, hey?" said the old gentleman. "Well, a nest egg is nothing to joke about, let me tell you. You'll find that out when you get older."

Just then Champ, who had been impatiently waiting for them outdoors, rushed up and began telling them that it was long past his dinner time, so they started home with him.

When they got out of sight of Doctor Holder's house, Djuna turned to Billy and said in an excited whisper:

"Did you see it?"

"See what?" said Billy.

"That egg!" exclaimed Djuna. "The one he couldn't remember the name of!"

"Of course, I saw it," said Billy, wonderingly. "What about it?"

"Didn't it remind you of anything?" demanded Djuna. "Didn't it make you think of something else?"

Billy pondered, and finally shook his head. "No," he said. "I don't know what you mean. What was funny about it?"

"Don't you remember that handle I showed you?" asked Djuna. "That funny round stone with the bird claw carved on it? Don't you remember?"

"Oh!" exclaimed Billy. "Oh, sure!" He began to look excited, too. "That's right, it looked just like that egg! Say, you don't suppose it could be the same thing, do you, with the claw taken off?"

"Of course not!" said Djuna decidedly. "It was a real egg, all right, the one in the box, I mean, and the other one was stone. But it's certainly queer, how much they look alike."

"Why don't you take that handle thing to Doctor Holder and show it to him?" Billy suggested. "I'll bet he could tell you about it."

"I can't," said Djuna. "It's gone."

Billy stared at him. "Gone?" he echoed. "Why, you showed it to me!"

"Yes, but it isn't there any more," said Djuna. "I don't know what's become of it. Somebody took it out of the bureau, after I showed it to you."

"For Pete's sake!" exclaimed Billy. "Well, it must have been Aunt Patty. Nobody else could have. Didn't you ask her?"

"No," said Djuna. "She was all worried about something else, so I didn't say anything to her about it. I guess she just took it to show it to somebody and forgot to tell me about it. It doesn't make any difference, I don't want it, anyway."

"Well, I would ask her if I was you," said Billy.

They walked on a little farther. Champ trotted on ahead.

"Do you suppose we'll ever find out who took Aunt Patty's boat and smashed it up?" asked Djuna in a discouraged tone.

"Gee, I don't suppose so," said Billy. "But what made you think of that?"

"I think of it all the time," said Djuna, gloomily. "I can't stop. But it doesn't do a bit of good. We didn't find any footprints, we didn't pick up anything, there just aren't any clues at all. They didn't keep the boat, and nothing was stolen out of the boat. There just isn't a single thing to show who did it. Not a thing!"

Billy shook his head. "I guess you're right," he said. "We don't even know what they were looking for."

Djuna plodded on, thinking hard. Suddenly he straightened up. "That's just it," he exclaimed. "Aunt Patty doesn't know why they took the boat away, but they must have been looking for something in it. That's what we've got to find out, first of all. If we can find out *what* they were hunting for, then we'll know *who* wanted it. Maybe."

Billy looked gloomier still. "I don't believe we'll *ever* find out," he said. "I don't believe anybody could."

"Well, I'm not going to quit," said Djuna. "No, sirree!"

And he took Champ home and gave him an extra big dinner, just to keep up his morale.

9. About a Pound of Sand

DJUNA SAT on the front step after supper, resting his chin in his hand, and trying to think of some way to solve the mystery, but it was no use. Clouds began to gather in the sky, and soon a few drops of rain fell. He went to bed early, and fell asleep listening to the rain steadily pattering on the roof.

When he woke up next morning, it was still raining. After they had finished their breakfast, Aunt Patty began to do some sewing, but Djuna did not know what to do with himself. It was raining too hard to go out. He wandered around downstairs for a while and then decided to go up to his own room and read a book which he had left lying on top of his bureau.

As he picked the book up, he saw the little bundle of old letters he had brought down from the attic several days before, and had forgotten about.

"My gollies!" he said to himself. "I forgot all about them!"

He untied the string around the bundle and opened the letters. There were only four of them. The first one was very short. It was written by someone who did not know how to spell. This is what it said:

deer siR I have Kleened out the EeGull Ness minE Yore oaN Biz Ness mi Wife an I doAN NeeD no Dark Ter

W. TUBBS

Djuna's eyes grew big as he read this strange letter. He guessed at once who had written it. The name signed to it, "W. Tubbs," must surely be that of Aunt Patty's husband, William Tubbs, who had been killed by falling from the big pine tree where the eagles' nest had been. "I have cleaned out the eagles' nest"—of course that meant that Mr. Tubbs had taken the last egg in the nest. But how could he have written the letter after falling from the tree? And why did he say that his wife—that meant Aunt Patty, of course—didn't need a doctor? Of course she didn't—*she* hadn't fallen out of any tree! Djuna shook his head wonderingly. He put the letter aside. He would have to study it more, later.

The next letter in the bundle was written very neatly, and not a single word was spelled wrong. But Djuna thought it just as puzzling as the first. It said:

Stony Harbor,
July 28, 1897

My dear Wife:

The eagles nest in stony harbor and what came from Patagonia must go to Patagonia.

AMOS GREENE.

Djuna read the strange message over and over again, but the more he looked at it the less he could understand it. At last he put it down and picked up the third letter. It was no less puzzling than the first two!

City Hotel, Broadway, New York,
August 7, 1858

My dear Wife:

I am distressed to find that I carelessly left behind me an object of considerable value. You know to what I refer. Please take great care of it till I return.

I am glad that little Amos was pleased by the curio. I purchased it in San Francisco from a miner who had obtained it while prospecting in the lofty Sierra Mountains. On reaching Canton, it occurred to me that a representation of it, if carved from some durable material, would form a most appropriate adornment. A skilful Chinese artisan was recommended to me, and when I had told him what I wished, he intelligently selected a stone exactly resembling it in color. For the foot, ebony was used. The workmanship is wonderful, as you can see.

I hope that you and our son are enjoying the cool breezes of Stony Harbor. The weather has been extremely warm in this city since my return. Expect me by Saturday's steamer.

Your husband,
H. GREENE

Djuna frowned, and began to read the fourth letter. It was much longer than any of the others. And this letter was the most puzzling of all:

Philadelphia
27th Nov^{br} 1795

My dear Wife:

I trust this letter finds you in the best of health, and I pray that I shall soon see you, my beloved Partner, an Event which will give me more happiness than any thing on Earth.

The violent Gales which we met off the Capes, obliging us to seek shelter in Delaware Bay, and thus prompting me to continue up River to this City, have now revealed themselves as a blessing from God, for here we have been able to dispose of our ship's cargo at a price higher than that obtainable elsewhere. Part of the money has already been paid over, and the remainder will be paid within a few days. I shall then be able to resume the voyage Homeward, to Stony Harbor, where, if your Emotions are equal to mine, our rejoicings will be complete.

As it is the duty of the Mate, of the Osprey, to supervise the unloading of our Barrels, I have seized upon an hour of leisure to walk about this wonderful Capital city and to view some of the streets. Learning that Mr. Wolcott, had been appointed a few months ago by President Washington to be Secretary of the Treasury, succeeding General Hamilton in that important post of Government, I made bold to call upon Mr. Wolcott and introduce myself. We discovered ourselves to be of exactly the same age. He welcomed me with every protestation of friendliness, as a fellow citizen of Connecticut, and flattered me by asserting that the Whaling Industry of Stony Harbor was of great importance in the commerce of our young Republic. Upon my remarking that I had brought back with me a pouchful of a heavy sand, in weight about one pound or more, obtained by trading with the natives of Patagonia, we having touched upon the coasts of that country on our return voyage from the whaling seas, Mr. Wolcott honored me by introducing me to Mr. Elias Boudinot himself. This Gentleman, who served our Country so devotedly during the late War, and who, being President of the Congress at the end of the War, signed the Treaty of Peace, was named by General Washington only one month ago to direct the business of providing our People with Moneys suitable to our needs as a nation. He received me at his offices, the very first buildings which have been erected especially for the business of Government. They are situated in Seventh Street, north of Market Street, on Sugar Alley, being very close to the house in which Mr. Jefferson lived at the time his pen inscribed the glorious words of our Declaration of Independence. You may well imagine the interest with which I gazed at that Edifice as I passed by it.

Upon being received by Mr. Boudinot, and exhibiting to him the sands I had brought from Patagonia, he informed me that their value was not less than 300 Dollars! When we are blessed with a child, let us set at least this sum aside, in the hope that it will increase. With this in mind, I will bring these same sands (though changed in appearance) home to you. Though not large in number, the Pieces will be of lasting value, and will mark the number of your years, reached upon your Birthday. To accomplish this fancy, I was obliged to confide to him the information that your age is five years less than my own. You may rest assured that he will keep this secret locked in his Bosom, for he is a Gentleman of the strictest probity. For the rest, he has promised that he will set about the work at once, and that it will be completed within the week.

I must now hurriedly bring this letter to an end, as the hour at which the Stage departs for New York is close at hand. The Gentleman to whose care I entrust this has assured me that he will place it on the first Stage leaving for Boston, after his arrival.

Your Husband,
BENJ. GREENE

Across the bottom of the letter was written, in another handwriting:

> Father's gift is still guarded. This day I have increased it, ten times.
>
> HIRAM GREENE, August 15th, 1858

When he had finished reading this letter, Djuna stood staring at it as if he couldn't believe his eyes. It was different from any book. Books talked about great men like George Washington as if they were a million miles away, and never made them seem real. But this was a letter written by Benjamin Greene, Aunt Patty's own great-grandfather, and he was talking about something George Washington had done "only a month ago." Why, it was almost as if George Washington was right there in Stony Harbor!

And there were a dozen queer things in the letter that were enough to make anybody wonder himself sick! "Sand," for one thing. What kind of sand could it be, that would be worth bringing all the way from Patagonia? Why had Captain Greene had to give the Indians anything for it? Why couldn't he have just scooped it up from the beach?

Djuna thought back about the story that Captain Atterbury had told him, about Captain Benjamin Greene's adventures in Patagonia. Captain Greene didn't get anything at all from the Indians in Patagonia, Djuna remembered. He was lucky just to get away from them without being killed. But, wait—hadn't he landed first in a country south of Patagonia? And wasn't that the place where he had traded with the Indians?

Sand! And why had Mr. Boudinot, the man who had been President of Congress, been so interested in it? That was another riddle!

Djuna wrinkled his forehead, trying to puzzle it out. He would *never* guess, unless he could guess how old Captain Greene's wife was.

But as he stared at the letter, Djuna's heart gave a sudden jump. What if that mysterious gift, "of lasting value," was the thing that the unknown robber was hunting for!

Gathering up all four letters, Djuna hurried downstairs to show them to Aunt Patty.

"Look!" he said excitedly. "Did you ever read these letters we found in the attic?"

"My gracious!" said Aunt Patty, putting down her sewing. "I thought the house had fallen down! Letters? What letters?"

"The ones we found in the sea chest," said Djuna. "Don't you remember?"

"Oh!" said Aunt Patty. "Oh, yes, I'd forgotten. No, I don't believe I ever looked at them. What are they about?"

"Well, just you look at them, Aunt Patty," urged Djuna, handing them to her.

Aunt Patty put on her spectacles and read all the letters carefully. She seemed to get more and more puzzled as she went on, shaking her head, and repeating some of the words out loud, as if she thought that might help her understand what they meant. The last one she read was the very short one that was signed "W. Tubbs," her husband's name. When she came to that, she flushed indignantly.

"Captain Tubbs never wrote that at all!" she exclaimed.

"I don't know what to make of it! He was a very good speller! Somebody else wrote it, and signed his name to it, just out of meanness! Why, it's dreadful!"

"But what does it mean?" asked Djuna. "Don't you know?"

"I don't believe it means anything at all," Aunt Patty declared. "It's just a lot of nonsense. Cleaning out an eagle's nest, indeed—why, nobody but a crazy person would think of such nonsense!"

"But how do you suppose it got into the attic?" Djuna persisted. "It was written to a doctor, you can see that, but why wasn't it sent to him?"

"It's all a mystery to me," said Aunt Patty. "The only doctor I know is Doctor Holder, and I wouldn't think of writing such a letter to him, and my husband wouldn't have written such a thing, either."

"Isn't that Mister Tubbs' handwriting?" asked Djuna.

"Certainly not!" snapped Aunt Patty. "You've seen his handwriting."

"Where?" asked Djuna, wonderingly.

"Why, on that scrap of paper you found," said Aunt Patty. "The one that said something about a nest egg. He wrote that. Oh, dear, I wish I knew what it all meant!"

Suddenly her eyes filled with tears, but she brushed them away.

"Gee, I'm sorry, Aunt Patty," stammered Djuna. "What's the matter?"

"Oh, nothing," she said, wiping her eyes. "It's just that there never *was* a nest egg in this house. Never mind, dear. I'll get along, somehow."

Djuna didn't know what to say. He felt embarrassed,

and sorry for Aunt Patty. He fidgeted from one foot to the other.

Aunt Patty looked at the letters again, and sighed. "I declare, I believe my own father must have been out of his mind when he wrote this one," she muttered, as she came to the one signed "Amos Greene." " 'The eagles nest in Stony Harbor.' Why, of course they did, when he was living. What a thing to say! And 'what came from Patagonia must go to Patagonia.' It just doesn't seem to make sense. As far as I can see, all my great-grandfather brought from Patagonia was a pound of sand!"

Djuna couldn't help giggling. "That wasn't worth very much, was it?" he said.

"No," said Aunt Patty, "not much."

She handed the letters back to him, and picked up her sewing again.

Djuna walked up and down the room, feeling very discouraged. What Aunt Patty had said about the nest egg reminded him of the carved stone egg, the old umbrella top, that had disappeared from his bureau drawer.

"Aunt Patty, I don't know what's become of that old umbrella handle Champ found up in the attic," he said. "I put it in the bureau in my room, and it's gone. You didn't take it, did you?"

Aunt Patty looked surprised. "Why, no," she said. "I haven't seen it since then. Are you sure you put it there?"

Djuna's heart sank. He knew now that he would have to face the fact that someone, not Aunt Patty, had gone into his room and taken the thing. But he didn't want to frighten her by saying so.

"Well, maybe I didn't put it there," he stammered. "Maybe I just thought I did. Maybe I left it somewhere else. I guess I'll go over and see if I left it at Billy's house."

Putting on his raincoat, he hurried over to have a talk with Billy.

Billy's mother came to the door, when Djuna knocked. "You'll find Billy down in the cellar," she told him. "He's being a detective, or something, I think."

Djuna went down the cellar stairs and found Billy standing beside the workbench there. In one hand he was holding a small square piece of glass and in the other hand he held a lighted candle. He was holding the piece of glass over the candle.

"For Pete's sake, what are you doing?" asked Djuna.

"Oh, hello, Djuna," said Billy, without looking around. "Look out, don't jiggle me. This is very important, it's got to be exactly right."

"Well, what is it?" said Djuna.

"It's to make fingerprints with," explained Billy. "You know, that's the way you can find out who committed the crime."

"What crime?" said Djuna.

"Why, any crime," said Billy, moving the candle flame around so that it got more black smoke on the glass. "That's the way the G men find out, with fingerprints."

"Say, that's right!" exclaimed Djuna, excitedly. "That's a swell idea! Have you got any fingerprints yet?"

"Well, I only started yesterday," said Billy. "I've got my mother's, and my father's, and Emmy's. That's them, over there, those three pieces propped up against the wall. Don't touch 'em, the smoke rubs off awful easy. And then I went over to the Harbor House and asked Mister Primrose if I could make his, but he said he would rather give me a nickel, so he gave me the nickel. And then I saw Harvey Bohnett and Bonehead, and I asked them, and they got mad, and said if I didn't mind my own business, they were going to tell my father on me. So then I came home and told him myself, and he said I'd better leave them alone. I was going to ask Phinny Truelove if I could make his fingerprints today, but it's so rainy I didn't want to go out. Is it still raining?"

"Well, it's just about stopped, now," said Djuna. "Look, I came over to ask you: let's go sailing, shall we? Let's sail over to Haypenny Island, shall we?"

"Well, sure, but let's wait till tomorrow," said Billy. "It's no fun when it's raining, and, besides, there isn't enough breeze. Gee, I hope the sun comes out and there's a good sailing breeze!"

"So do I!" said Djuna.

10. Champ and Djuna Dig In

As DJUNA and Billy had hoped, the next morning was sunshiny, and a fine breeze was blowing across the harbor. Djuna ate his breakfast as fast as he could, and then, with Champ scampering along at his heels, he hurried to Billy's house. Billy was already waiting for him at the wharf, and his boat was rocking up and down at the landing float as if it was impatient to start. All the rain water that had fallen into it the day before had been emptied out, and Billy had taken a big sponge and mopped up the last drops of it, so that it was as dry as could be. After Champ had been made to climb into his special place of safety in the bow, the boys hoisted the sails and the boat fairly raced down the harbor and was headed out across the glittering expanse of water.

Although it took them an hour and a half to reach the two little islands, every minute of the sail was exciting, for the wind blew hard, the spray dashed in their faces, and every boat they saw in the distance might easily have been a pirate ship.

Steering in between the two islands, they lowered the sails, then pushed the boat up the narrow channel leading to their secret cove, where they anchored. After helping Champ to get ashore, where he scampered off to explore the island, they went swimming in the cove. Then they put on their sneakers and climbed to the top of Eagle Rock, where they sat until the wind and sun had dried them off.

"I'll tell you why I wanted to come over here especially," said Djuna. "I wanted to see if there was anything left of that eagles' nest."

"Left of it?" exclaimed Billy. "Why, that pine tree blew down so long ago, there isn't even anything left of the tree!"

Djuna pointed at the ground below them. Looking down on the island from the top of the rock, it was easy to see that most of the grass and bushes on the island grew in a sort of wide path that stretched from Eagle Rock across to the sandy beach on the other side. Nearest the beach was a little hump of ground where the bushes grew thickest of all.

"You see that sort of path the bushes make?" said Djuna. "Well, I'll bet that's where the pine tree fell. Then it rotted away little by little, and the grass grew up all around it, more than any place else. And out there at the end, where that little bump is, is where the top of the tree came, with the nest in it. Eagles' nests are awful big.

I saw a picture of one, once. They're almost as big as a haystack, made out of sticks and things. I'll bet that's where it is, all covered up with dirt. Let's go and look."

"Gee, I guess that's what happened, all right," said Billy, eagerly. "But there can't be anything left of the nest, by now. The sticks would rot away, too, wouldn't they?"

"I suppose so," Djuna admitted. "Let's look, anyway."

Champ had been wandering along the beach, barking at seagulls whenever they flew past him, and chasing after them till he came to the edge of the water, but they stayed well out of reach and just laughed at him. When he saw the boys climbing down from the rock and walking across the island, he hurried over to join them.

"I wish we had brought something along with us to dig with," said Djuna. "Maybe we could find some Indian arrowheads, or something."

"Or treasure!" exclaimed Billy. "I'll bet pirates used to come here and bury treasure! This would be a dandy island for pirates!"

He looked around for something to dig with, and picked up a broken piece of board that had floated ashore on the beach. It wasn't much use, as a spade, and after trying for a while to dig into the mound of earth which, Djuna thought, probably showed where the eagles' nest had fallen, he gave it up and threw the board away.

But Champ had decided that this was a very exciting game, the sort of game he liked best. He began digging away furiously with his front paws, at the hole that Billy had started. The dirt flew. The boys laughed at him and started to walk away.

"He probably thinks he's going to dig out a woodchuck,

or something," said Djuna. "He used to do that, when we lived in Edenboro."

Just then Champ began barking angrily, and the boys turned around to see what was the matter. He was still digging away at the hole and had uncovered something that looked like the end of a round stick. He was trying to pull it out with his teeth, but it was stuck too fast. Djuna thought that Champ had probably found an old bone.

"Here, wait a minute, Champ," said Djuna. "I'll help you."

Djuna tugged at it, but it was buried so deep that he finally had to get the board that Billy had used and scrape away some more of the dirt before he could pull the stick out. He was surprised to find that it was more than two feet long. At one end it was almost as big around as a baseball bat, but it gradually tapered to the other end, which was not much thicker than a thumb.

"Why, it's a cane!" exclaimed Djuna. "For Pete's sake, look what Champ found!"

"Get the dirt off of it," urged Billy. "Let's see what it looks like."

Champ jumped up and down, begging for it, but they wouldn't let him have it. Taking it over to the cove, they carefully washed off the dirt that had stuck to it, and found it was made of a beautiful yellowish white bone, like ivory. The thicker end of the cane was hollow, like a bamboo fishing pole, making a tube several inches deep. Around and around the inside of the hollow part, at the top, were deep grooves, so that a plug could be screwed in.

Djuna looked at Billy. Billy looked at Djuna. And

then they both nodded their heads very solemnly, looking a little scared.

"That's what it's for!" said Billy. "That stone egg was the top of this cane!"

"It couldn't be anything else!" said Djuna.

"But Aunt Patty said it was an umbrella handle," said Billy.

"I knew all the time it couldn't be," said Djuna, "as soon as she said her grandmother was a little bit of a woman. It was much too big for an umbrella handle."

"Did you find out if Aunt Patty took it?" asked Billy.

Djuna shook his head. "I asked her," he said, "and she said she never touched it. But I'll bet I know who it was, now."

"You do?" exclaimed Billy. "What was it?"

Djuna looked all around and then whispered something in Billy's ear.

Billy looked doubtful. "Oh, no!" he exclaimed. "Honest?"

"I don't see how it could be anybody else," insisted Djuna. "But I'm going to make sure just as soon as we get back. You just wait."

"Do you think that's who took Aunt Patty's boat, too?" whispered Billy.

"I don't know," said Djuna. "This cane wasn't in the *Patagonia*, anyway. It's been lying there where Champ found it, for years and years. And that's the funniest part of it, too. It never would have got there if the eagles hadn't carried it up to their nest, first."

"The eagles?" exclaimed Billy, scornfully. "What are you talking about?"

"Of course it was the eagles," Djuna insisted. "One

of them must have seen it lying on the ground somewhere and thought it would make a good stick for the nest. When the tree fell, it fell with the nest. How else could it have happened? You know perfectly well that nobody would have brought it all the way out from Stony Harbor, just to hide it in the ground, like that. Do *you* think they would?"

"Well, no," Billy admitted.

Djuna walked up and down, thinking hard. "No, sir," he said at last, "that old letter shows that this cane used to belong to Aunt Patty's grandfather. But the cane doesn't have anything to do with the reason why Aunt Patty's boat was stolen, because the cane was buried here long before the *Patagonia* was stolen."

"Old letter?" exclaimed Billy wonderingly. "*What* old letter?"

"Why, I told you," said Djuna. "One of those old letters that were in the attic."

"Oh!" said Billy. "I remember you told me you found some, but I never saw them. If I come over to your house, can I see them?"

"Sure," said Djuna. "Let's start home now, shall we? I'm starving to death!"

"So am I!" said Billy.

It took them almost two hours to sail home, and by the time they got to Billy's house, they were hungrier than ever. Billy's little cousin, Emmy, was standing on the wharf and ran down to meet them when they reached the landing float.

"Where have you been?" she demanded excitedly. "I've been looking all over for you, and I couldn't find you anywhere!"

"Oh, we've been sailing," said Billy.

"*I* had a birthday," said Emmy, importantly. "You just ought to see the presents I got! We had ice cream, too!"

"Oh, boy!" said Djuna. "Is there any left?" asked Billy, eagerly.

"I guess so," said Emmy. "Mother saved some for you, in the icebox. That's what I came over to tell you."

Both boys started running for Emmy's house, with Champ at their heels. Emmy's mother laughed when she saw them at the kitchen door. But she gave them each a big plateful of ice cream. When they had finished it, Emmy showed them the presents she had been given for her birthday.

"And I got a nest egg, too," she said proudly.

"A nest egg!" exclaimed Djuna. "I didn't know you had any chickens!"

Emmy looked puzzled. "I haven't got any chickens," she said.

"Then what are you going to do with the nest egg?" asked Djuna.

"I'm going to keep it, of course," said Emmy. "That's what it's for."

"What good is a china egg?" asked Djuna. "I mean, if you haven't got any chickens?"

"I guess you don't know what a nest egg is," said Emmy. "Look, I'll show you."

Going to the table where she kept her postage stamp album, she brought back a small flat book. She spread it open in front of Djuna.

"There!" she said. "That's the nest egg my mother gave me! My mother says if I don't spend it for a whole year, it will grow into two!"

Tucked between the leaves of the book was a paper dollar. Djuna stared at it and slowly grew red in the face.

"Gee, why didn't I think of that before?" he stammered. "There's two different kinds of nest eggs, of course!"

Billy jumped to his feet, looking excited. "Maybe that's what that piece of paper meant, Djuna!" he exclaimed. "It said something about hiding a nest egg, didn't it? And you said a nest egg was just a china egg. Maybe it meant hiding *money!*"

Djuna looked more ashamed of himself than ever. "I know," he said. "That's probably just what it meant, but all I could think of was a *china* nest egg!"

Emmy looked from one boy to the other. "What piece of paper are you talking about?" she said. "You don't ever tell me anything!"

"Well, it was just a piece of paper we found up in Aunt Patty's attic," said Djuna. "There was just a little piece that the mice, or the squirrels, or something, hadn't chewed up. It was about a nest egg, but it didn't say anything about hiding the nest egg—what it said was, 'I have put the nest egg where it belongs.' "

"I put *mine* where it belongs," said Emmy. "I put it in the money part of the book. The first part of the book is about stamps, and the rest of it is about money, so that's where I put my dollar."

Djuna picked the book up again and read the name printed on the outside. It was called: "THE UNITED STATES STAMP & COIN CATALOG." Djuna began to look through it. The beginning of the book had pictures of postage stamps in it. Then, as Djuna kept on turning the pages, he came to a page which had pictures of pennies on it. Another page had pictures of nickels—five-cent pieces—on it. Then came pictures of dimes, and of silver half-dollars, and silver dollars, and of all the different kinds of money.

"Gee, this is a dandy book!" said Djuna. "Where did you get it, Emmy?"

"Oh, a man gave it to me," said Emmy.

Djuna kept on turning the pages. Suddenly a strange look came over his face. He sat staring at the page as if he had seen a ghost.

"Hey, come on, Djuna," said Billy, impatiently. "Aren't you ever going to stop looking at that book? I'm hungry!"

Djuna jumped, as if somebody had waked him out of a sound sleep. "Huh?" he said. "Oh, all right, all right, I'm coming. I was just thinking, that's all."

He shut the book and handed it back to Emmy. "That's a swell book," he repeated. "Do you suppose I could get one like it? From the man that gave it to you, I mean. Who was he?"

"Oh, just a man," said Emmy. "He came here and asked my mother if she had any old furniture or anything to sell. And I was fixing my stamp album, so he asked me if I wanted a book about stamps, and he gave me this book. He was awful nice."

"For Pete's sake, Djuna!" exclaimed Billy. "Aren't you ever coming?"

"Oh, all right," said Djuna. "Thanks a lot for the ice cream, Emmy."

He followed Billy outdoors, but when they got to Billy's house Djuna hesitated on the doorstep.

"Say, I think I'll go on home, Billy," he said. "Be sure and tell Mr. Primrose about the fingerprints, will you? I'll see you tomorrow."

"What's the matter with you?" exclaimed Billy. "Aren't you going to eat?"

"Oh, I don't want anything now," said Djuna. "I've got to go home and do some work. I just don't feel like eating anything, thanks."

And taking the cane that Champ had dug up on Haypenny Island, he hurried off, followed by Champ, leaving Billy staring after him in astonishment.

"This is something we've got to think out by ourselves, Champ," said Djuna, after they got home, and he had tied Champ up in the woodshed. "You do your thinking in the woodshed, and I'll give you an extra big dinner tonight."

Djuna was very busy indeed all the rest of that afternoon. The first thing he did was to go to his room, get out the package of old letters, and read them over and over, very carefully. The next thing he did was to go to the Public Library, which was a small gray stone building covered with ivy vines, in the middle of a little park. He took with him a list of five questions he had written out and handed them to the librarian.

"Could you help me find the answers to these, please?" he said.

The librarian read the questions and then looked at Djuna in astonishment.

"My gracious!" she gasped. "You'd better sit down. This is going to take a long time."

These were the five questions Djuna had written out:

1. How old was Mr. Wolcott, the Secretary of the Treasury, in 1795?
2. What was the first house built in Philadelphia by the United States Government?
3. What sort of valuable sand was found by the Indians south of Patagonia?
4. What big bird made its nest in the high mountains of California?
5. What is a nest? I don't mean a bird's nest.

"My gracious!" said the librarian again. But she began looking in different books, and in a few minutes she had found all the answers, because she knew the right books to look into. She wrote them down on the piece of paper, and when Djuna read them he grew so excited that he could hardly keep from shouting out loud.

"Thanks a lot!" he said. "Oh, gee, thanks an awful lot!"

On the way home, he stopped at Emmy's house, and asked her if he could look again at the book with the pictures of stamps and money. "And have you got a ruler to measure with?" he asked.

Emmy got the book and a ruler, and Djuna turned over the leaves of the book until he came to the page he was looking for. He measured the width of one of the pictures on the page. Emmy was bursting with curiosity.

"What in the world are you doing?" she asked, dancing up and down.

Djuna grinned. "It's a secret," he said. "I can't tell you, right now. But I will, just as soon as I can, cross my heart."

"Oh, I think you're just as mean as you can be!" wailed Emmy.

"Well, I'm in a hurry," said Djuna. "I'll tell you later, don't worry!"

When he got home, he mystified Aunt Patty, too. He borrowed her tape measure, emptied her spools of thread out of the box where she kept them, and measured the inside of the box, without telling her why he was doing it. Then he took the tape measure out to the woodshed, where he had hidden the cane he had brought home from the island, and measured the top of the cane, inside and out.

After that, for another hour or two, he sat in his room, frowning at a piece of paper on which he had written down everything he could think of that might have anything to do with the mysterious things that had happened since he came to Stony Harbor.

"There's just one thing missing," he muttered to himself. "Well, I'm going to ask Doctor Holder. I guess he knows more about birds than anybody else."

He hurried over to Doctor Holder's house and rang the bell. The old gentleman came to the door.

"Could I please ask you a question?" said Djuna breathlessly.

"Why, of course, my boy," said Doctor Holder, "What can I do for you?"

"Well, it's about that eagle we saw," said Djuna. "That bald eagle, I mean. Can you please tell me if that's the only kind of eagle that there is around here? Is there any other kind?"

Doctor Holder smiled. "That's very odd," he said. "That's the second time I've been asked that question lately. Yes, the bald eagle is the only true eagle in this section of the country. People see turkey buzzards and fish hawks occasionally, and think they are eagles, but they aren't really. They don't belong in the same group."

"Thanks very much," said Djuna. "That's all I wanted to know. But did you say somebody else asked you the same question?"

"Why, yes," said Doctor Holder. "Just a day or so ago. Some stranger, who wanted to see my collection of eggs. I'm sorry, but I don't recall his name."

"Well, thanks a lot," repeated Djuna. And he hurried back home.

When he took Champ's dinner out to him, he looked very thoughtful.

"I've got an awful lot to do tomorrow, Champ," he said, patting the little black dog. "You stay here and take care of Aunt Patty till I get back, do you hear?"

11. Djuna Learns from Alberto

As SOON as he had finished breakfast the next morning, Djuna started for Billy's house. But first he went around to the dingy little hotel, the Harbor House, creeping up the alley that led to the back of the hotel, and keeping carefully out of sight of anyone who might be on the front porch. Peering in the kitchen door, he saw Mr. Primrose, the colored man, and gave a low whistle to attract his attention. Mr. Primrose came over to the door.

"Did you take them up to their rooms?" whispered Djuna.

"Yes, suh, I sure did," whispered Mr. Primrose. "I put them right on the little tables, right alongside of their baids, just like Mister Billy told me. You want to see 'em?"

"No, not now," said Djuna. "But don't let anybody else see them. Are they up yet?"

"No, suh," said Mr. Primrose, grinning, "they is sleeping like babies."

"Okay," whispered Djuna. "We'll be back pretty soon."

He hurried on to Billy's house. As soon as Billy saw him, he could tell that Djuna had something important to tell him.

"Listen!" said Djuna, excitedly. "You know who the Count of Monte Cristo was, don't you?"

"Sure," said Billy. "He was a sailor, and he found a box full of diamonds and everything, on an island, and he got rich. Why?"

"Well," said Djuna, "so is Aunt Patty! We're going to help her so she can be *Mrs.* Count of Monte Cristo! Hurry up, let's get started!"

Billy stared. "Started for where?" he said.

"For Sixpenny Island, of course!" said Djuna impatiently. "Have you got a spade, or a shovel, or something?"

"My golly!" exclaimed Billy, commencing to get excited. "Is there a box of diamonds out there? Do you know where it's buried?"

"It isn't a box of diamonds," said Djuna. "I never said a word about any diamonds. But, gee whiz, if we don't start right away, we might be too late! I'll tell you about it while we're sailing over there, everything I found out. Where's the spade?"

Billy ran and got the spade from the cellar, and then both boys ran down to the wharf and tumbled into

Billy's boat. They were in such a hurry to hoist the sails that they got the ropes all tangled up, and had to start all over again.

"It's a good thing I didn't bring Champ along this time," said Djuna. "He'd get in your way even worse than I do."

They got the mainsail hoisted. Billy ran back and took the tiller. "Stand by to hoist the jib," he commanded. The breeze was coming strong and steady from the southwest. "We'll go out on the port tack," he said. "Hoist away!"

Djuna hoisted the jib, made the halyards fast, and took charge of the jib sheets. The boat moved slowly away from the landing float and soon began to gather speed, as Billy trimmed in the mainsheet. They crossed the harbor on the port tack, then came about and headed straight for the islands on the long windward reach. Djuna got the jib to pulling just as Billy wanted it, and then settled himself beside Billy in the stern sheets to tell him what he had been doing, and why he had decided that on Sixpenny Island they would find the answer to the whole mystery. The boat seemed to jump from wave to wave, cutting its path swiftly through them. Billy watched the sails steadily, but as he listened to Djuna's story his eyes sparkled.

"Oh, boy!" he exclaimed. "*That lantern!* When are you going to tell the police?"

"Just as soon as we get back," said Djuna. "But I thought we'd better do this first. I haven't told Aunt Patty a single thing about it, yet. Gee, I thought that if I told her, and then we came over here and couldn't find anything at all, it would be awful!"

"I sort of wish we'd asked my father to bring us over

here," said Billy, uneasily. "What if they followed us out here and caught us?"

"Oh, don't worry," said Djuna confidently. "They'll never think of it. I'll tell you what we'd better do, though —we'll hide the boat in our secret cove, and you stay on guard there and keep a lookout. I can do the digging by myself, and then I'll call you. But if you see a boat coming, you come over and tell me. Okay?"

Billy agreed to this plan. Soon they reached the narrow channel separating Sixpenny and Haypenny Islands, lowered the sails, and paddled the boat into the tiny cove sheltered by Eagle Rock. Djuna got into his swimming trunks and went back to the channel, taking the spade with him. He waded out as far as he could, and then had to swim only a few strokes before his feet touched bottom again, and he was able to wade the rest of the way to the beach of Sixpenny Island.

The roofless cabin that had once belonged to Captain Tubbs, Aunt Patty's husband, stood right at the edge of the beach. Djuna walked toward it, the water squishing out of his wet sneakers. He looked back once, to see if Billy was watching him. But the steep slope of Eagle Rock hid Billy and the boat completely from sight. He went on.

Peering cautiously around the corner of the cabin, Djuna saw no one anywhere. The deserted island lay sleeping peacefully in the sun. Nothing stirred, except the leafy branches of the old lilac bushes, moving in the breeze.

Djuna stole up to the sagging door of the ruined hut and listened. But there was no sound except the crying of the seagulls flying overhead.

Reassured, he went on in. The one room was half in darkness, for boards had been nailed across the windows, on the outside; but so much of the roof was gone that Djuna could see patches of blue sky overhead, and a shaft of sunlight streamed slantingly across the dusty floor.

Djuna went straight to the fireplace.

Ashes were heaped thick upon the brick hearth. During the many years when the cabin had stood empty, fishermen had now and then built fires of driftwood in the fireplace, but no one had ever bothered to clear away the ashes. The rusty old iron kettle in which they had steamed clams still stood there at one corner of the fireplace, and around it were heaps of the empty clam shells.

Djuna began to shovel away the ashes with his spade, heaping them against the sides of the fireplace. Soon the brick floor came in sight. Djuna's heart gave a jump.

In the center of the floor was a flat stone, about a foot square. Letters were carved in it.

Djuna brushed the dust away, eagerly. The words cut in the stone were these:

"KEEP THE NEST WARM."

Djuna seized his spade again and excitedly set to work. Loosening the bricks around the stone, he lifted them out one by one. Then, with the edge of the spade, he pried up the stone.

Underneath it lay a small box of dark wood, about the size of a cigar box.

Small as it was, it was surprisingly heavy. Djuna tugged, lifted it out and put it down near the old kettle.

For a moment he hesitated. Then, deciding to cover up the stone again, he lifted it back, put the bricks back in place around it, and began to shovel the ashes back on top of the bricks. He was so excited, and was working so busily that he was deaf to the sound of a motorboat that came quietly up to the beach, paused a moment, and then went away again.

Too late, he heard footsteps coming toward the cabin. He looked around wildly. There was no way of escape. There was no door except the front door. Frantically, he threw a shovelful of clam shells over the box he had taken from the fireplace, and then bounded to the other corner of the room.

With his back to the wall, he faced around, desperately hoping that the footsteps would pass by.

But they came straight on, to the door. A man shouldered his way in.

Djuna's heart sank. The intruder was "Bonehead" Bohnett.

A startled look spread over the man's stupid face as he saw Djuna.

"What are you doin' here, kid?" he demanded, taking a step toward him. "My brother Harve is a-lookin' for you! You and that smarty friend of yours, that kid Reckless!"

"You mean Billy?" asked Djuna innocently. Only one thought was in his mind—he must keep Bonehead from finding out that Billy was anywhere near them, and alone! "I haven't seen him for a long time." And to himself he added, "Not for almost an hour!"

"Well, how did you git out here?" demanded Bonehead. "How did you git here on Sixpenny?"

"I swam here," said Djuna, truthfully. He was sure, from Bonehead's question, that Bonehead had not seen Billy's boat, hidden in the secret cove.

Bonehead grunted. "Swam over!" he said, scornfully.

"You tryin' to tell me you swum three miles, from Stunny Harbor? You think I'm a fool?"

"I didn't say that, Mister Bohnett," said Djuna politely. "But if you don't believe me, just look at my swimming pants. I swam here, I tell you."

Bonehead looked doubtful, and rubbed his chin. "Well, you're goin' to stay right here, anyways," he said, "until my brother Harvey comes. *He*'ll fix you!"

"Where is your brother?" asked Djuna, desperately.

"Now, wouldn't you like to know?" drawled Bonehead provokingly. "Maybe he's gone over to Stunny Harbor to fetch a friend of ourn, and maybe he ain't. Maybe when he gits back the three of us will haul up some of old lady Tubbs' lobster pots, and maybe we won't. Maybe we'll git ourself a good lobster dinner, and maybe we won't. I ain't tellin'. What do you reckon I brung these rubbers for? To ketch eagles with?"

Grinning, he showed Djuna what he held in his hand—a small cardboard box full of elastic rubber bands, very short and sturdy rubber bands.

Djuna knew only too well what they were for—they were the bands which the fishermen put around the claws of live lobsters, to keep the claws from pinching them. He flushed angrily. Bonehead and his brother were planning to rob Aunt Patty's lobster pots!

Bonehead chuckled. "Now, don't ye git mad," he said. "Take it easy!"

Bonehead sat down at the doorstep of the cabin and stretched his long legs out. He filled his pipe and lit it. He looked lazily off to sea, instead of watching Djuna. But as Djuna could not have got outdoors without stepping over Bonehead's legs, Bonehead hardly needed to watch him.

"Might as well make yourself comf'tubble," said Bonehead. "It'll be a long time, mebbe, before Harve gits back."

"Do you mind if I walk around, Mr. Bohnett?" asked Djuna, wretchedly.

"Walk around all you're a mind to," said Bonehead, grinning. "Only don't go tryin' to climb out. I wouldn't do that, if I was you. You might get hurted."

He puffed away at his pipe without looking around. Djuna hated the sound of his voice. For a moment he stood looking angrily at the back of the man's head. His fists clenched. But then he dropped them despairingly. What was the use? The man was so big and strong that it was useless to think of trying to get away from him!

Djuna walked up and down the sagging floor boards of the cabin, his thoughts racing wildly. What could he possibly do? No one but Billy knew where he was, no one knew that he had been made a prisoner, no one would come to rescue him. . . .

He stopped short, and almost gave a groan. He bit his lip, choking down the lump in his throat. No one coming? Why, it was worse than that—Billy might get tired of waiting for him and come to look for him, at any minute!

Yes, Billy would come, and he would walk right into the trap! There was no way to warn him!

Djuna could see just how it would happen, just as plainly as if it were already happening right before his eyes. Billy wouldn't guess that anything was wrong, he would come sailing around from Haypenny Island, and anchor and come ashore, and come running up to the hut, never once dreaming that anyone except Djuna would be there. And Bonehead wouldn't make a sound, nor let

Djuna shout a warning, but would squat there, silent as a tiger, until Billy had walked up to the shack, and then he would pounce on him!

Djuna felt more worried about Billy than about himself. He must save Billy from capture, but how could he possibly do it? It was dreadful to feel so helpless. He gritted his teeth. One thing was sure, he desperately resolved—if he heard Billy's footsteps coming toward the shack, he would shout! No matter what Bonehead might do to him, afterwards, he would shout! It wouldn't give Billy much time, but perhaps it would save him. There was nothing to do, now, but wait, and hope!

As he walked back and forth, staring at the floor, he tried his best to think of some way in which to head Billy off, so that he would not come!

He glanced up at the rafters. There was plenty of room between them to throw a stone, for the roof itself was gone. He remembered how Billy and he had tossed stones down through it, that day they first visited Eagle Rock. He looked around, trying to find something that was neither too large nor too small, to throw. He saw the old iron oarlock and picked it up. But it was much too big and clumsy to throw. He tossed it aside, discouraged.

And besides, he told himself, what would be the use of attracting Billy's attention by throwing stones towards Billy's boat, even if he had any stones to throw? If they hit near the boat, they would make Billy yell, and Bonehead would hear him. Or, if he didn't yell, he would come over to see what was the matter, and then Bonehead would grab him. Either way, it would be useless, or worse than useless.

No, he would simply have to think up some way to

write a message and some way of getting it to Billy. But how could he possibly do such a thing?

There wasn't a chance! The whole idea was so hopeless that Djuna felt like screaming. Write a message? Why, he wasn't even wearing anything but his swim suit! He had the stub of a lead pencil in his shirt pocket—but his shirt was back there in the locker of Billy's boat! Even if he had had a pencil, there was no paper to write on! Nothing!

He looked down. There on the floor lay the tattered old almanac. He picked it up and began turning over its pages, just because he couldn't think of anything else to do.

There was a calendar for each month of the year printed on each page, with the days of the month, and the hour when the sun rose each day, and when it set, and all such information. Djuna had turned over three or four pages before he noticed that at the bottom of each page were printed some words that had nothing to do with the date or the weather. The words he first noticed at the foot of the page were these:

WORDS WORTH REMEMBERING

Capt. Lawrence said, Don't give up the ship!
Chickens always come home to roost.
It pays to get an education.
Always help others.
The quickest way to end a quarrel:
Never begin one.

"Don't give up the ship!"

Those were the words that Djuna saw first. He straightened up. It was as if someone was shouting encouragement to him, just when he had given up hope. "Never surrender! Don't give up the ship!"

Courage rose again in his heart. He read the brave command over and over. It comforted him. He would *never* give in, now! Somehow, somewhere, he must find a way!

He stared at the rest of the sentences on the page. Well, he thought, they held good advice, but they didn't help to cheer him up, just now. . . . They didn't help him. . . . And, then, just as he was about to turn the page, he gasped. Why, yes, they *could* help him! A look of wonder and surprise and eagerness spread over his face. Yes, perhaps this was the way to escape! "Don't give up the ship?" No fear, he wouldn't!

His eyes darted eagerly from object to object on the disordered cabin floor—the pile of clam shells, the old boot that Champ had dragged across the floor, the heavy oarlock, shaped like a rounded Y; and, last of all, the open package of rubber bands that stood there on the floor by the doorway, close to Bonehead's hand!

He caught Bonehead's eyes on him, watching him.

Carelessly, as if he had found nothing in it to interest him, Djuna tossed the almanac on the pile of clam shells. He walked toward Bonehead, smiling.

"Gee, Mr. Bohnett, I'm getting tired of being in here," he said, pleadingly. "Can't I go outdoors and run around a little?"

Bonehead shook his head. "No, you'll be all right here," he drawled. "Why don't you set down and rest your legs, the way I'm doin'? Don't cost ye nothin'."

Djuna sighed. "Well, all right," he said. He bent over and picked up the cardboard box of rubber bands.

"Do you mind if I look at them, Mr. Bohnett?" said Djuna. He tried to make it sound as if it didn't matter at all.

"Go ahead," said Bonehead amiably, relighting his pipe. "Only don't ye lose none of 'em, 'cause we'll probably need all of 'em, me and Harvey."

"Oh, I won't," said Djuna, and added under his breath, "At least I hope not."

Taking the rubbers with him, he squatted down beside the pile of clam shells, with his back to Bonehead, so that what he was doing could not be seen.

With swift fingers, he picked up the printed almanac and tore out the lower part of the page he had been looking at. Folding the edges of the scrap of paper carefully, he tore it twice across, along the creased lines, making three pieces of it. Quickly selecting an empty clam shell from the pile, he slipped one of the three pieces of paper into the hollow halves of the shell, and just as quickly snapped a rubber band around the shell, closing it tight. In a jiffy he had slipped the shell into his canvas sneaker, and under the arch of his foot.

He was just in time. Bonehead had risen to his feet and was strolling over to see what Djuna was doing.

"What in tarnation are ye tryin' to do?" he asked, peering over Djuna's shoulder.

Djuna looked up.

"I was just wondering how I could make a slingshot out of these rubbers," he said dolefully. "But I guess I can't—they're too short to do anything with."

"Slingshot, hey?" said Bonehead. "Well, now, that's an idee! Used to have a lot o' fun with a slingshot, myself. Here, lemme see them bands."

He took a handful of them from the box, and turned them over in his powerful fingers.

"They're too short," Djuna repeated. "I was wondering how I could tie some of them together, but I haven't got any string."

"String?" said Bonehead. "What do ye need with string? You ain't much of a hand at knots, I reckon. Here, lemme show you."

Taking two of the bands, he slipped one end of one band through the other band, then deftly pushed the end of the second band through the other end of the first one. Then he pulled them tight, and held them up triumphantly for Djuna to see. They were knotted into one, a band twice as long as it had been.

"Gee, that's swell!" exclaimed Djuna. "But they'll have to be even longer than that, I guess. Do you think you could make them longer, Mr. Bohnett?"

Bonehead beamed. "Easiest thing in the world!" he said. "Just gimme some more of 'em." And forgetting all about his own warning not to lose any of them, he knotted one band to the other until he had two sizeable strings.

"There!" he said, proudly. "There you be! But what are ye goin' to use for the crotch? Haven't got one here, have ye?"

"I thought I'd use that oarlock over there," said Djuna, pointing at it. "It's about the right size, isn't it?"

"Why, sure," said Bonehead, picking it up. "This is bigger than most—must have been for a scullin' oar, in a whaleboat, likely. Sure, this ought to do fine!"

"And for the leather, I thought I'd cut a piece out of that old boot," said Djuna innocently. "But we still need a piece of string to tie it together with."

"Oh, so you were goin' to cut it, was ye?" asked Bonehead sarcastically. "What with? Don't see any knife around here, do ye? Or was ye fixin' to chew it off?"

Djuna was meekly silent, while Bonehead fished a knife from his own pocket, grinning. Hugely delighted with his own fun, Bonehead cut a wide strip of leather from the old boot and punched holes in each end of it with the point of his knife blade.

"You see?" he said. "Ye don't need any string—just pull the rubber through these holes and knot it the same way. Now ye can fasten it to the oarlock with a couple more of them rubbers, and there you be!"

He handed the finished slingshot to Djuna and went back to his seat by the open door. "What are ye aimin' to shoot at?" he asked, as he refilled his pipe and lit it again.

"Oh, nothing," said Djuna. "Can I go outdoors and see what I can hit with it?"

"No, sirree!" said Bonehead emphatically. "If I was to let ye go out on the beach, you might signal to somebody goin' by. Right here is where you stay, till my brother gets here. And don't you git to thinkin' you can fool me into lettin' you loose, nohow."

Djuna made no answer. Pretending to sulk, he went back to the empty fireplace and the piles of clam shells beside it, and made several "bullets" by stretching rubber bands around empty shells, to hold them shut. Standing with his back to the fireplace, he made practice shots with them, and was delighted to find that the home-made slingshot sent them straight and far. They whanged up against the opposite wall of the cabin with thuds that satisfied him that they would have easily carried across the narrow channel to Haypenny Island and the hidden cove where Billy was waiting.

When he was sure of this, he took the first shell that he had made and put it in the sling. Then, pulling the rubber back as far as he could stretch it, he aimed into the air and let go. The shell flew up into the blue sky, framed by the bare rafters, higher and higher, then curved downward.

Djuna drew a long breath and turned towards Bonehead, who had been yelling with delight at each shot as it hit its mark.

"Don't you want to try it now, Mr. Bohnett?" he asked. "It's really a dandy!"

"Yeah, wouldn't ye like me to?" retorted Bonehead, with a sly wink. "Nothin' would suit ye better'n to git me foolin' with that thing, so as you could git away when I wasn't watchin'. No, sir, you don't fool me that easy, young feller!"

"Well, I just thought you might like to try it," said Djuna meekly. "I don't see why you should think I'd want to fool *you*, Mr. Bohnett. You've helped me a lot, you really have!"

"Don't try to soft-soap *me*, young feller," said Bonehead sternly. But Djuna could see that he was much pleased by the flattery.

Djuna wandered around the cabin, whistling carelessly. But each time he passed the boarded-up window on the side nearest Eagle Rock, he paused. There was a crack between two of the boards, through which he could get a glimpse of the channel between the two islands. The fifth time he peered through the cracks, he saw what he had been hoping for—the white sails of Billy's little boat, silently gliding away from the island.

After that, every minute seemed like an hour.

Djuna sat down on the dusty floor and tried not to worry. But he couldn't help worrying. It would take Billy almost two hours, perhaps, to get to Stony Harbor. Perhaps he wouldn't get there at all—perhaps Harvey Bohnett's motorboat would meet him, and stop him. Perhaps the wind would die out. Perhaps—

Suddenly Bonehead jumped to his feet, grinning. "Here comes Harvey!" he chuckled. "Heerd his whistle!"

Djuna stood up and drew a deep breath. He had been thinking hard, and he had already decided what he must try to do if Harvey Bohnett arrived before Billy could get back with help. He must try to delay the two brothers just as long as he could!

Harvey swaggered in. And behind him came the black-haired man that Djuna had first seen at Mr. Truelove's store, and then at the Harbor House.

"Got him right here for ye, Mister Patina!" said Bonehead gleefully, pointing at Djuna. "There he be!"

Djuna hurried forward before the two newcomers had had time to open their mouths.

"Gee, I'm glad you got here, Mr. Patina!" he said eagerly. "I went around to the Harbor House this morning to tell you we've found the eagles' nest, but they said you were asleep, so I got Billy Reckless to bring me out here right off! He went back to tell you. Didn't you see him?"

"Naw, we didn't see him," growled Harvey Bohnett, suspiciously. "Don't lie to me, kid! Where is he?"

He took a step toward Djuna, but the black-haired man seized his arm.

"No, leave him alone, Harvey," he said impatiently. "The nest! The nest! Where is it, boy? Quick!"

"It's on Haypenny Island," said Djuna. "It's where the tree fell down, the big pine tree, where the nest was. It's all heaped up there, and there's grass growing all over it, but you can tell that's where it was. Want me to show you?"

"Come on, Bohnett, hurry!" exclaimed Mr. Patina, tugging at Harvey's sleeve. "Come along, boy. Show us where it is!"

"Now, hold your horses," growled Harvey. "You say it's buried, kid? Didn't you dig it up?"

"We didn't have any spade with us when we found it," Djuna explained. "We tried to dig it up with an old board, but we couldn't. We brought a spade today, but I haven't dug any there, yet. I was waiting for Billy to get back, so he could help."

"What did you do with the spade?" exclaimed Patina, excitedly. "Where is it?"

Djuna pointed to the spade, which was lying where he had dropped it, beside the old rusty kettle by the fireplace. He held his breath, scarcely daring to breath, while Mr. Patina rushed over and picked up the spade. But Mr. Patina saw nothing else, except a fireplace heaped with ashes and an old kettle full of empty clam shells.

The black-haired man hurried back with the spade, and Djuna's heart stopped thumping. He started to walk carelessly toward the door. Harvey Bohnett seized him by the arm.

"You're goin' to stay right with us till we git through with you," he growled. "No use your tryin' to git away."

"Why should *I* try to get away?" exclaimed Djuna, innocently. "I'm having a swell time, Mr. Bohnett!"

But as they marched him down the beach and ordered him to get into the Bohnetts' motorboat with them, Djuna looked anxiously across the water toward Stony Harbor, longing for the sight of a rescuing vessel on its way toward him. But there was no sign of one. Even Billy's boat had disappeared from view, and Djuna felt a sudden chill of fear. What could have happened to Billy?

"Don't give up the ship!" he repeated to himself. "Don't give up the ship!"

Bonehead threw off the mooring lines from the rickety pier, and Harvey steered the motorboat towards Haypenny Island. Djuna tried desperately to think of some way to gain time. As they came opposite the channel between the two islands, he jumped up.

"Look!" he exclaimed. "There isn't any good place to land on Haypenny Island, unless you go up this channel! There's a creek that goes into a little cove, that's the best place, right by Eagle Rock!"

Harvey scowled over his shoulder. "Don't tell *me* how to run my boat!" he snapped.

"Do what the boy says!" ordered Mr. Patina sharply. "It will save time, won't it?"

"It certainly will!" said Djuna. And under his breath he added, "For *me!*"

Harvey muttered, but steered the motorboat up the channel and into the cove. They climbed ashore.

"Now, then, where is the nest?" Patina demanded. "Show me where it is, boy!"

Djuna led the way across the island, till they came to

the hump of earth, covered with low bushes, where he and Billy and Champ had found the ivory cane.

"There it is!" he said.

Mr. Patina began digging furiously. The sun blazed down on them, and it was hot work. In ten minutes Mr. Patina grew tired and handed the spade to Bonehead. Bonehead dug until the sweat poured down his face, then handed the spade to his brother. The hole grew deeper and deeper. Next, Harvey took up the digging. Minutes passed, and still the spade turned up nothing except bits of rotting twigs, that showed where the nest might once have been. Djuna sat with his chin on his hands, staring anxiously across the water toward Stony Harbor, but no boat came. He grew more and more worried.

Suddenly Harvey Bohnett stopped working and straightened up, listening intently, his hand cupped behind his ear.

"What's that?" he exclaimed. "Hear it?"

They all listened. In a moment, the sound was plain—the sound of a powerful motorboat, growing steadily louder. It was coming, not from Stony Harbor, but from the opposite direction. A moment later, the motorboat came into sight, traveling so fast that a cloud of white spray was thrown back from her bows. She was coming straight towards them.

"That's the Coast Guard boat!" exclaimed Harvey, his voice shaking with terror. "Git back to our boat, quick!"

All three men took to their heels, running toward the cove. Djuna stayed where he was. He saw them scramble over the rocks, fling themselves on board, and try to start the boat. Then howls of rage floated back to him.

They were trapped. The tide had started to ebb, just

as the boat entered the cove. So much water had run out, while they were digging, that the boat was stranded.

As the Coast Guard launch came closer, Djuna ran down to the beach and waved his arms frantically. When it was opposite him, he saw Billy Reckless among the men on the launch, waving wildly at him. The next minute, the launch slowed down and came slowly toward him. He ran to meet it, splashing out till he was waist-deep. A rope came flying out to him. He grabbed it. Strong hands hauled him on board.

"Are you all right?" asked Billy anxiously.

"Sure," panted Djuna, "as soon as I get my breath!"

The officer in charge of the launch, a bos'n's mate, patted him on the shoulder.

"Now, young man," he said, "what's this all about?"

Djuna pointed toward the cove. "There's a boat in there, with three men on it," he said. "They're the ones that stole Mrs. Tubbs' boat and wrecked it! I got them to go into the cove, but I guess I forgot to tell them the tide had started to run out. I guess they're stuck there, or something."

The bos'n's mate threw back his head and roared with laughter. "You win!" he chuckled. "*You* don't need the Coast Guard!"

"Well, they'll only be stuck there about ten hours," said Djuna seriously. "Could you please arrest them before the tide comes back?"

The bos'n's mate roared again. "Well, I guess we can get around to it," he said, wiping his eyes. "You seem to want them pretty bad."

"Yes, sir," said Djuna. "Look, I don't think there's enough water left in that channel for your boat to get in there, but you won't have to. There's an old pier around on the other side of Sixpenny Island you can moor up to, and then you could just holler over to them and make them wade over there."

"You seem to have it all figured out," chuckled the officer. "We'll see if we can get them for you that way. But are you sure you can prove they're the men that stole Aunt Patty's boat? You'll get in trouble, you know, if you can't prove it."

"I can prove it," said Djuna confidently. "Do you want me to tell you how?"

When he had explained how he meant to prove it, the officer stared at him in admiration, and then solemnly stuck out his hand.

"Well, put her there, mate!" he said. "Shake! Blow me down, if I don't believe you can do it! I'll back you up, and that's my word of honor! Let's go!"

He gave the order to proceed to the landing place on Sixpenny Island. After that, until they got there, he only shook his head and mumbled, "Wait till the wife hears this!"

But he didn't smile. He didn't smile even when Djuna suddenly said, "Oh, gee, I almost forgot—they took Billy's spade over there!" He just shouted across the channel, "Come over here, you three, and bring that spade back with you!" He didn't smile at all when the three men came wading and stumbling across the channel, looking frightened to death, and were lined up in front of him. The crew of the launch closed in around them.

"I've got evidence that you three are the men that stole the *Patagonia* from Mrs. Tubbs and wrecked it," said the officer sternly. "What have you got to say for yourselves?"

Mr. Patina laughed scornfully. "Say?" he repeated. "Why, I say that's ridiculous! We were at the Harbor House that night, all three of us, and we can prove it!"

"That's right!" said Bonehead eagerly. "Nobody seen us take it!"

"Shut up, you!" snarled his brother. "Anybody that says they seen us take it is a liar!"

"That will be enough out of you!" said the Coast Guard man sharply. He motioned to Djuna. "What's *your* story, Admiral?" he asked. "Tell us what you know."

"Well, this is what happened that night," said Djuna slowly, looking straight at Bonehead as he spoke. "You and your brother came to Mr. Truelove's wharf in your boat, and you stayed there and talked to him until after it got dark, didn't you?"

Bonehead nodded.

"And then," Djuna went on, "you told him you were going to the Harbor House, and you got into your boat and went away, didn't you?"

"Don't answer him!" growled Harvey Bohnett.

"But you didn't go to the Harbor House," said Djuna. "You just went as far as the middle of the harbor, and shut off your engines and your lights, and waited there, in the dark."

No one said a word.

"And then *you* sneaked past Mr. Truelove's wharf in the dark!" cried Djuna, suddenly pointing at Mr. Patina. "He didn't hear you, because he was inside his store, listening to the radio. You tiptoed out on the next pier——"

"That's a lie!" squealed Mr. Patina, pale with fear and fury. "I never went there!"

Djuna laughed. "You went out on the pier," he said

quietly. "You untied the *Patagonia's* mooring lines and dropped them. You climbed down into the *Patagonia* in the dark. You knew there would be somebody waiting there to help you."

Mr. Patina's eyes seemed starting from his head. "Nobody was there!" he said in a hoarse whisper. "You're crazy! I wouldn't know how to start the engine!"

"The Thing that was helping you didn't need any engine," said Djuna. "It didn't make any noise. It just moved in the dark, and carried the *Patagonia* along with it. It was the tide, going out, and it took you out to the Bohnetts' boat."

Mr. Patina wiped the sweat from his forehead. He tried to laugh. "So that's it, is it?" he said. "That's a likely story! You had better be careful, my boy, you're going to get into trouble if you say things like that!"

Djuna paid no attention to the interruption. "The reason you wanted to get the *Patagonia* away from the wharf," he went on, "was because you thought that Mr. Tubbs had hidden some money in it before he died, and you wanted to hunt for it. So you hired Harvey Bohnett to help you."

"I ain't going to stand for this!" Harvey burst out angrily. "I ain't never been near old lady Tubbs' boat!"

"Oh, is that so?" said Djuna calmly. "Well, you three can settle that between you. You wouldn't let Billy take your fingerprints, but we got them, anyway."

"Nonsense!" exclaimed Mr. Patina. "What are you talking about?"

"Fingerprints," said Djuna. "We put some smoked glass in your room at the Harbor House yesterday, when you weren't there, and last night you left marks all over it. We got fingerprints from all three of you."

All three of the men looked down quickly at their hands. Harvey swore. Bonehead put his hands behind his back. Mr. Patina laughed nervously.

"Well, what of it?" he demanded. "What if you have got my fingerprints? That doesn't prove I had anything to do with stealing that boat!"

"Yes, I think it will," said Djuna pleasantly. "You see, I happened to find that lantern still burning, on the *Patagonia*, and the chimney glass was all smoked black. You can get awful good fingerprints on smoked glass, you know."

Bonehead suddenly looked as if he were going to cry. "My gosh, Harve," he wailed, "I told you we hadn't ought to light that there lantrun!"

Harvey Bohnett's fist swung at Bonehead savagely. "Shut up!" he yelled. "It wasn't me that lighted it, it was Patina!"

The Coast Guard crew laughed till the tears ran down their cheeks. Holding his sides, the officer at last managed to stop laughing and to command silence.

"That's enough!" he gasped. "Take these three pirates over to the station and have 'em locked up! They're as guilty as goldfish, by their own confession. Then bring Captain Reckless' yacht back here with you, and don't tow her too fast, or you're apt to strain her planking. Take it easy, and by that time we ought to be able to get that boat out of the cove. I'll wait here with the boys till you get back. I want to hear more about this. I haven't had so much fun since the night before Christmas!"

When Mr. Patina and the Bohnett brothers, still shaking their fists at each other, had been marched on board the launch and taken away, Billy and Djuna and the bos'n's mate strolled up to the tumble-down shack together.

"Say, tell me one thing, Admiral," the officer said to Djuna as they walked along, "did you really find a lantern on board the *Patagonia*? Were there really finger marks on it?"

"Why, of course," said Djuna. "It's hanging up in Aunt Patty's woodshed. But I didn't say there were finger marks on it. I just said you *can* make fingerprints on smoked glass, and that's true. Billy made a lot of them, and that's what made me think of it."

"And there really were some on the lantern chimney?" persisted the bos'n's mate.

"How could there be?" exclaimed Djuna, in surprise. "The chimney couldn't get smoke on the outside, it was just on the inside. But I was pretty sure they wouldn't think of that."

"No," said the bos'n's mate, looking at Djuna with new respect, "they wouldn't think of that. But what made *you* think of it?"

Djuna looked embarrassed.

"I wouldn't have thought of it if it hadn't been for Billy," he said. "Billy didn't have a dog, so he could name him Alberto, he just *had* to have one! So he made him up. And we just *had* to have some fingerprints. You can do almost anything when you have to, I guess. Alberto can."

"And besides," he added thoughtfully, "I was pretty sure Bonehead wouldn't notice. He sits down on chairs when they aren't there."

12. The Eagles' Nest

ON THE doorstep of the shack, Djuna picked up the slingshot that he had got Bonehead to make for him.

"This old thing worked all right, didn't it, Billy?" he said proudly. "It must have, or you wouldn't have gone for help. How close did that clam shell come to you?"

"Gee, it scared the life out of me!" said Billy. "I was just sitting there, wondering why you didn't come back, when, all of a sudden, *wham!* it came right down *kaplunk* in the bottom of the boat and bounced right out again! It had just started to sink when I grabbed it. As soon as I opened it up and found that message in it, I snuck out of there just as fast as I could. Say, where did you get that piece of paper, anyway?"

Djuna looked around on the floor by the fireplace and found the two scraps of paper he had torn out of the old almanac.

"Here," he said, "let me have that piece you've got there. It fits in between these other two pieces, like this."

The three pieces, put together, read like this:

Capt. Lawrence said   Don't   give up the ship!
Chickens always   come   home to roost.
It pays to   get   an education.
Always   help   others.
The   quick   est way to end a quarrel:
Never begin one.

"Don't come, get help quick!" muttered the bos'n's mate, reading the middle words downward. "Oh, boy, oh, boy! And you mailed it in a clam shell!"

"Well, I didn't have any postage stamp," said Djuna, giggling, "and, besides, if I'd mailed it with a stamp, Billy wouldn't have got it till the next day."

Billy and the Coast Guard officer laughed, but Billy kept looking around the empty cabin, searching for something. Djuna watched him with a mischievous smile on his face.

"What are you looking for, Billy?" he asked innocently.

"The treasure, of course!" exclaimed Billy. "Didn't you find it?"

The Coast Guard officer looked startled. "Hey, what did you say?" he exclaimed. "Treasure? *What* treasure?"

The boys looked from one to another. Djuna nodded.

"I guess I'd better begin at the beginning," he said.

He led the way outdoors, and they sat down in the shade of the old lilac bushes.

"The way it began," said Djuna, "was really when I was in Edenboro. I live at Miss Annie Ellery's house in Edenboro, all winter. This summer, Miss Annie got a letter from Aunt Patty Tubbs. Aunt Patty said in the letter that she was in trouble, and she wished she had somebody to stay with her. So Miss Annie sent me to live here with Aunt Patty in Stony Harbor for a while, and she let me bring my dog, Champ, with me. Miss Annie told me to find out what sort of trouble Aunt Patty was in, if I could, but not to bother Aunt Patty with a lot of questions. And it's turned out that it was lucky I brought Champ, too!

"Well, I talked to people who knew all about Aunt Patty, and they all said that she wasn't in any trouble now, except she was poor. They all liked her and were sorry for her, but they didn't like her husband, before he got killed, a long time ago. It was really Mr. Tubbs that was to blame because she was poor, but she always gets mad if anyone says so.

"Then, all of a sudden, the funniest things began to happen! The funny thing was that they were all mixed up with eagles and eggs! Champ found a stone egg, with spots on it, and an eagle's claw holding it, up in the attic. Aunt Patty said it was an umbrella handle, but it wasn't. I put it in my bureau drawer, and the next time I looked for it, it was gone. Billy and I found a piece of paper in the attic, and it said on it, 'I have put the nest egg where it belongs.' I thought that a nest egg was a china egg. I didn't know it could mean money, too. I asked Aunt Patty if she ever had a nest egg, and she said no. You see, I was thinking about a china egg, and she thought I was talking about money.

"The same day that the stone egg was stolen, Aunt Patty's wooden darning egg was stolen. It's a hollow wooden egg, as light as a feather.

"Before that, Billy and I saw an eagle over there on Eagle Rock—a real, live eagle. All the feathers on its head and neck were white. That's the kind of eagle that's called a bald eagle. Billy and I went to see Doctor Holder, and he showed us a bald eagle's egg. It's white. It hasn't got any spots on it at all.

"And then Aunt Patty's boat, the *Patagonia,* got stolen. The funny thing about that was that those three fellows didn't want the boat, and they didn't want anything they found in it! They forgot what boats are for. Boats are for carrying things across water.

"Aunt Patty said they hadn't stolen any money, because she never had any money to steal."

The Coast Guard officer wiped the sweat from his forehead. "I've heard of mysteries before," he said, "but this has got them *all* beat!"

"Yes, sir," said Djuna. "That's what I thought, too. And after we found the letters, it was worse than ever."

"Letters?" said the bos'n's mate. "What letters?"

"We found them in the sea chest in the attic," explained Djuna. "Aunt Patty's great-grandfather wrote one of them, and her grandfather wrote one, and her father wrote one, and Mr. Tubbs wrote one. Two of them talked about eagles' nests, and, of course, I thought they meant the nests the eagles used to build in the pine tree on Eagle Rock. The letters just got me mixed up worse than ever. I got Billy to bring me over here to hunt for the nest, and all we dug up was an old hollow bone cane that my dog found. Do you know what that cane was? No, wait, I'd better explain something else, first!

"I guess I just never would have found out about the treasure, if it hadn't been for Billy's cousin, Emmy. She's got a book, with pictures of coins in it. As soon as I saw it, I went home and read those old letters again, and then I went to the Public Library and got the lady there to help me, and all the pieces began to fit into each other, just like a jigsaw puzzle!

"Aunt Patty's great-grandfather was the captain of a whaleship. He landed on the coast south of Patagonia. He traded with the Indians there, and got some sort of heavy sand from them, about a pound of it. I found out at the Library what it was. It was gold dust! * He got back to Philadelphia with it. He took it to the Mint.** The Mint is the place where they make coins. They told him it was worth three hundred dollars. His wife was thirty years old,*** so with the three hundred dollars he bought thirty gold coins, worth ten dollars apiece, from the Mint, brought them home to his wife, and asked her to keep them for a nest egg.

"That was all in the first letter, the one Captain Benjamin Greene wrote. At the bottom of that letter, his son,

---

* In the description of Argentina (which includes Patagonia) in the Encyclopedia Americana, Vol. II, page 11, it is said that "in the territories of Tierra del Fuego and Santa Cruz, and along the Atlantic coast, the sands, especially after great storms, contain an abundance of gold dust."

** The Philadelphia Mint, built in 1792, was the first public building erected by the United States Government. The first American gold coins were made there in 1795.

*** Oliver Wolcott, Secretary of the Treasury, was born in 1760. Captain Benjamin Greene, Aunt Patty's great-grandfather, was born the same year, and was therefore 35 years old in 1795, when he wrote the letter. His wife was five years younger than he.

Captain Hiram Greene, wrote sixty-three years later that the gift was still guarded, and that he had increased it ten times. That meant that he was saving three hundred and thirty gold coins, worth ten dollars apiece, for the nest egg."

The bos'n's mate sat up straight. "Zowie!" he exclaimed. "Three thousand, three hundred dollars! That ain't hay!"

Djuna nodded. "No, sir," he said. "But Aunt Patty had told me that she never had had a nest egg. If there was any money, she didn't know where it was. Maybe it had all been spent. Captain Atterbury told me that Aunt Patty's father spent all his money, and didn't leave any to Aunt Patty.

"Then I read the next letter. Captain Hiram Greene wrote it. It was about something he had given his little boy, Amos. Well, I guessed right away what that was, because Doctor Holder showed us a great big spotted egg that he said Amos Greene gave him. The letter said that Captain Greene bought it from a miner who got it in the mountains in California. So that was another thing I asked about at the Public Library, and the lady showed me a book about birds, and it said that the kind of eagle that lives in the high mountains in California is the golden eagle, and it has spotted eggs!

"Yes, sir, a golden eagle! It's bigger than the one we saw, the one that nests here! It has dark brown feathers, almost black, but the old ones have feathers that look like gold, at the back of their heads!

"But, listen! Did you know that a ten-dollar goldpiece is called an eagle? *I* never knew that, till I saw that book of Emmy's!

"So that made me think of something else in that letter.

That's just what that spotted stone looked like, the golden eagle's egg, with the eagle's claw holding it. And after we found that hollow cane, I was sure that the stone egg was made for the handle of the cane. I measured the hollow part of the cane. It was wide enough and deep enough to hold *thirty* gold eagles!

"But where did Captain Greene keep the *three hundred* gold eagles? I kept saying to myself, 'They were a nest egg, a nest egg, he wanted them to hatch into *more.*' And all of a sudden I remembered a little box that Aunt Patty keeps her sewing things in. It's got a cover, and it says on the cover, 'Hatch & Hatch.' Aunt Patty said it had belonged to her mother, or maybe to her grandmother, and they always had kept spools in it. It had a velvet lining. The velvet was dented, pressed down in little circles. Aunt Patty said the spools made the dents. I didn't see how they could, I didn't think spools of thread would be heavy enough. But a stack of ten gold eagles would be about the same size as a spool, and it would be much heavier. I measured inside the box. There was room enough there for three hundred and twenty gold eagles!

"But that wasn't any use. They weren't there! It wasn't even any use asking Aunt Patty, because she had never even heard of them.

"The only thing that I was sure of was that they had kept the gold eagles in the cane, when they had only thirty of them. But, after Captain Greene got three hundred more, they had to put them in the spool box, most of them, anyway. But that still left about a dozen that they kept in the cane, until Mr. Tubbs got a bigger box and took them, too, and threw the stick away after he came to the island. As soon as I get the top of the cane back, I'm going to put it on the stick and give it to Captain Atterbury, because he said he would like to have it.

"By that time, I had figured out where the eagles had been kept, at first, but I still didn't know what had become of them, after they had been taken out of the cane and out of the spool box. I had to study the letters some more.

"There was one letter that Aunt Patty's father had written. All it said was, 'The eagles nest in stony harbor and what came from Patagonia must go to Patagonia.' I got to thinking about it. The more I thought about it, the more I thought there was something queer about it. There never was any eagles' nest in Stony Harbor, in the village—the only one was out here on Haypenny Island, and that's three miles from Stony Harbor. Aunt Patty's father didn't mean they nested in a village. He meant the nest was in a harbor of stone. 'What came from Patagonia' meant the gold. When he said it had to go to Patagonia, he meant that it had to go to Aunt Patty, because that's her name.

"Gee, I was getting pretty excited, then, because that meant that he *hadn't* spent all the money, the way people said he had, but was keeping it for a nest egg for Aunt Patty, when she grew up. Where had he hid it? What was a harbor of stone?

"I asked the lady at the Public Library if there are any kind of nests that aren't birds' nests. She looked in a great big book, a dictionary, I guess, and she said any snug, cozy sort of place is called a nest, and a place to put things is called a nest. So then I tried to remember what Captain Atterbury told me about Aunt Patty's father, and I remembered he said he used to sit by the stone fireplace and tap his cane on the floor and say, 'All I've got left is right here!' A fireplace—gee, that's the cosiest place in a house! And it was stone, Captain Atterbury said. A stone place, where you put things!

"And then I got to thinking about Doctor Holder. Aunt Patty said her mother and father liked Doctor Holder an awful lot, just as if he was their own son, before she was born. After they died, he took care of the nest egg for her until she got married to Mr. Tubbs. He didn't like Mr. Tubbs, and when he took the money back to Aunt Patty, he buried it in the fireplace for her, just where her father had kept it. He wrote a letter to Mr. Tubbs and said, 'I have put the nest egg where it belongs,' and told Mr. Tubbs to keep it there. Mr. Tubbs got mad, and wrote a letter to Doctor Holder and told him to mind his own business, and was going to mail the letter to him, but Aunt Patty wouldn't let him.

"Mr. Tubbs dug up the nest egg, just the same. He said in the letter, 'I have cleaned out the eagles' nest.' Of course he didn't say in the letter where he was going to put the eagles. But when I asked Aunt Patty what had become of the stone, she said Mr. Tubbs had taken it over to his cabin on this island. He tried to get her to come and live over here, with him, but she wouldn't. So after that he climbed up the pine tree to the eagles' nest and fell off and broke his neck.

"I think Aunt Patty is awful nice about Mr. Tubbs. She knows he took the nest egg, so she says she never had any nest egg. She knows he wrote that letter to Doctor Holder, but she says somebody else must have written it. You know what I think? I think that next to Miss Annie Ellery she's the nicest person there is!

"Well, anyway, the day that the stone egg got stolen out of my bureau drawer was the same day that Aunt Patty's wooden darning egg got stolen. The front door was open, and nobody was home, not even my dog Champ. There's a gray squirrel that lives in a tree right next door. It came into the front room and found that darning egg on the floor and carried it off. Champ and I found the darning egg a couple of days after that, lying on the ground, under the tree. It had squirrel teeth marks on it.

"But the squirrel couldn't have gone upstairs and opened my bureau drawer and carried off the stone egg.

"Aunt Patty said four people came to see her that morning, one at a time. One was Mr. Truelove, one was Captain Atterbury, one was Billy's cousin Emmy, and one was a junk man who wanted to buy old paper. Well, afterwards I told Billy that a junk man came to buy old paper, and he said there isn't any junk man in Stony Harbor.

"The next time I heard about the junk man was when I was looking at Emmy's stamp catalog. She said a man came and asked her mother is she had any old paper to sell. He gave her the stamp catalog. His name was printed right on the catalog. It said, 'Julius L. Patina, Dealer in Rare Stamps and Coins, Hoboken, N. J., U. S. A.' "

"Patina!" exclaimed the Coast Guard officer. "That's the man we just arrested?"

"That's the man," said Djuna. "The first time I ever saw him was the day after I came to Stony Harbor. He was talking to Mr. Phinny Truelove, in Mr. Truelove's store. He bought overalls for two dollars and twenty-three cents and gave Mr. Truelove a twenty-dollar bill. Mr. Truelove counted out the change. He gave him a five-dollar bill and two one-dollar bills, and a quarter, and two pennies, and a half-dollar, and another half-dollar that was the same color as a new penny. At least, I *thought* it was a half-dollar."

"A gold eagle!" exclaimed Billy. "Was that what it was?"

"I guess so," said Djuna. "I guess Mr. Patina kept it. Well, anyway, he stayed at the Harbor House, and he went around asking everybody if they had any old junk up in their attics to sell, and pretending he was a junk man. I guess what he was looking for was old postage stamps, on old letters, because Stony Harbor is an awful old town. I saw him talking to Harvey Bohnett and Bonehead one day, but I didn't think anything about it, then. And all the time he was trying to find out where there were some more gold eagles, but, of course, I never thought of that until I saw that book he gave Emmy. And then there was hardly any time left. They had already tried to find out if Mr. Tubbs had hidden them on board of the *Patagonia*. The next place they would look would be here in this cabin where Mr. Tubbs used to live. There wasn't any time to lose. I thought Billy and I could get over here and get home again before they came, but they got here too quick. When Mr. Patina came in, I was so scared that the only thing I could think of was to tell him we had found the eagles' nest on Haypenny Island, and he was so greedy that he never stopped to ask questions. Gee, it certainly was lucky!"

"What do you mean, 'lucky'?" said the bos'n's mate, admiringly. "I know better! *You* don't have to depend on luck. You just think faster than the other fellow, that's all! But, say, didn't you find the treasure before they got here?"

"Of course," said Djuna. "But I didn't have time to count them. I'd just got them dug up when Bonehead came."

"For Pete's sake!" said Billy, "are they still right there where anybody can see them?"

"Come on, I'll show you," said Djuna, jumping up. He led the way into the cabin and pointed toward the fireplace. Billy and the Coast Guard officer stared at it.

"Where?" said Billy. "I don't see anything except that old kettle full of clam shells."

"Well, that's all that Bonehead saw," said Djuna. "I dumped the clam shells in there just before he came in."

The bos'n's mate stared at it, shaking his head. "Don't tell me any more, Admiral," he said hoarsely. "That's wampum!"

"Let's take it to Aunt Patty just like this!" said Billy. "Shall we?"

"Oh, gee, that's a swell idea!" said Djuna. "Boy, will she be surprised!"

"You don't mind if I come along, do you?" asked the bos'n's mate respectfully. "The wife will be sore if I don't give her the final bulletin."

"Oh, sure!" said Djuna, eagerly.

In a few minutes the Coast Guard launch came into sight towing Billy's boat behind it, and Billy and Djuna carried the rusty old iron kettle down to the rickety wharf, between them, because it was pretty heavy. The

Coast Guard crew helped them lift it into the launch. The bos'n's mate remembered to bring the spade along, and they all got into the launch.

"Excuse me, chief," said one of the crew, touching his cap to Djuna. "That black-haired guy, that Patina guy, he asked me to give you this. He said to tell you he was sorry he ever took it."

He handed Djuna the spotted stone egg with the eagle's claw on it.

"Oh, thanks very much," said Djuna. "I was pretty sure he took it, when Doctor Holder said a man had been asking him about eagles. So I asked Mr. Primrose, he's a colored man that works at the Harbor House, and he said he had seen it in Mr. Patina's room, but we didn't have time to get it, then."

The bos'n's mate took the launch around to Haypenny Island and left two of his men there, with orders to bring the Bohnetts' boat to the Coast Guard station as soon as the tide came in. Then they headed for Stony Harbor, still towing Billy's boat, and in half an hour they had reached the wharf at Billy's house. They tied the launch and Billy's boat at the landing float and went ashore. The first person they saw was Billy's father, who had just finished mending and painting Aunt Patty's boat, the *Patagonia.* When he looked up and saw Billy and Djuna coming towards him, stumbling along with the heavy kettle between them, and four Coast Guard men in uniform marching behind them, he nearly dropped the paint pot in his astonishment.

"Hey, dad, come on!" yelled Billy. "We're all going to Aunt Patty's!"

Captain Reckless put down the paint pot and hurried over to ask the bos'n's mate what the boys were up to. The bos'n's mate laughed, and asked him to come along and see, so Captain Reckless came along.

Billy's mother stuck her head out of the door and nearly fell off the porch.

"Come on, Mom!" yelled Billy. "We're all going to Aunt Patty's!"

Emmy and her mother came running out of their house.

"Hey, Emmy, come on over to Aunt Patty's as quick as you can!" yelled Djuna.

Emmy and her mother hurried to catch up with the procession.

When they went past the Harbor House, Mr. Primrose, the colored man, woke up out of a sound sleep and joined the crowd.

Mr. Steptoe, the fish-store man, saw them coming and yelled across the fence to Mr. Phinny Truelove, who was sitting in the shade in front of his store.

Mr. Truelove shouted to old Mr. Jackson the fisherman, who was mending a net on the next wharf, and Mr. Jackson limped up to join the crowd as fast as he could.

By the time they got to Aunt Patty's back door, there was hardly room for everybody in the little back yard. Billy and Djuna put the kettle down on the garden path. The path was made out of clam shells; all the garden paths in Stony Harbor were made out of clam shells. Djuna unfastened the woodshed door and let Champ out. Champ ran around and around, barking so hard that he shook all over.

Djuna dashed into the house and ran into the front

room and almost bumped into Aunt Patty, who had just got up from her chair and was coming to see what the noise was about.

"Djuna, where *have* you been?" said Aunt Patty. "You haven't had any lunch! But I've saved some for you. Wait, I'll get it right away! But what on earth is all that noise out there?"

Djuna pulled her toward the kitchen door and threw it open. "Come on, Aunt Patty," he whispered, "you've got some callers!"

As she got to the door, they all cheered. "Hurrah for Aunt Patty!" they shouted. "Hurrah! Hurrah! Hurrah!"

Aunt Patty turned pale and put her hand on the door. "Merciful goodness!" she gasped. "What's this all about?"

Djuna and Billy, standing side by side in front of her, were trying hard not to laugh at the joke they had planned.

"Now, watch us, Aunt Patty!" said Djuna. "We brought some clam shells to fix the path with! Look!"

They both bowed to her, very solemnly, and then lifted the old iron kettle and spilled the clam shells out on the path. The last thing to fall out was a small wooden box, resting on top of the heap of shells. Djuna bent over and lifted it. Small as the box was, it was so heavy that he could lift it only with both hands.

"Why, for Pete's sake!" exclaimed Billy, pretending to be terribly surprised. "What's that?"

"Surprise!" yelled Djuna. "Surprise! Chickens come home to roost, and eagles come home to nest! This is for *you*, Aunt Patty!"

He got as far as the kitchen table, and the heavy little box slipped out of his hands. It burst. Showers of gold, rockets of gold, cascades of gold, jumped and streamed and flashed and gleamed everywhere, spreading over the table and ringing to the floor like a musical rain.

Aunt Patty picked up one of the golden disks. She looked at it. She put it down and clasped her hands.

"Djuna," she said in a trembling voice, "go down to Phinny Truelove's store and buy all the ice cream he's got! I'm going to give a party!"

* * *

When all the gold eagles had been picked up, and counted, and stacked on the table in neat piles, and everybody was sitting around, eating ice cream in different flavors, and Champ had been given a special bone to take out to the woodshed, Djuna winked at Billy and nodded toward the door, and the two boys quietly slid out without being noticed. After they got around the corner of the house, Djuna walked on for a little way without saying anything. He looked worried.

"Look," he said finally, "I got a letter from Miss Annie Ellery this morning. She says she wants me to come back to Edenboro."

"Gee!" said Billy. They walked on for a while in silence.

"I wish I could stay all summer," said Djuna.

"So do I," said Billy. "Maybe you can come back."

"Well, maybe I can," said Djuna hopefully. There was another silence.

After a while Billy sighed.

"Gee," he said, "Alberto's going to miss Champ a lot!"

T72. BUFFALO BILL, Shannon Garst	50¢
T73. SUE BARTON, SENIOR NURSE, Helen Dore Boylston	35¢
T74. TOUCHDOWN TWINS, Philip Harkins	50¢
T75. THE BLACK ARROW, Robert Louis Stevenson	50¢
T76. THE GREAT HOUDINI, Epstein and Williams	50¢
T77. THE KID COMES BACK, John Tunis	35¢
T78. BEYOND ROPE AND FENCE, David Grew	35¢
T79. WOLF DOGS OF THE NORTH, Jack Hines	35¢
T80. SCARLET ROYAL, Anne Emery	35¢
T81. BEST SHORT SHORTS, Eric Berger, ed. (Jan. 1958)	35¢
T82. YUKON MYSTERY, Joseph H. Gage (Jan. 1958)	35¢
T83. BIG RED, Jim Kjelgaard	35¢
T84. YELLOW EYES, Rutherford Montgomery	35¢
T85. WE SHOOK THE FAMILY TREE, Hildegarde Dolson	35¢
T86. YOU'RE ASKING ME? Gay Head	35¢
T88. PROM TROUBLE, James L. Summers	35¢
T89. THE GREEN TURTLE MYSTERY, Ellery Queen, Jr.	35¢
T90. NATIONAL VELVET, Enid Bagnold	50¢
T91. FOR GIRLS ONLY, Sylvie Schuman, ed.	35¢
T92. THE PRINCE AND THE PAUPER, Mark Twain	50¢
T93. SHAG, Thomas C. Hinkle	35¢
T94. PRAIRIE COLT, Stephen Holt (Dec. 1958)	35¢
T95. WILD HORSE TAMER, Glenn Balch (Feb. 1959)	35¢
T96. BLACK BEAUTY, Anna Sewell (Jan. 1959)	50¢
T97. SORORITY GIRL, Anne Emery	35¢
T98. GOLDEN EAGLE MYSTERY, Ellery Queen, Jr.	50¢
T99. CROSSWORDS FOR TEEN AGERS, M. Rockowitz	35¢
T124. TO TELL YOUR LOVE, Mary Stolz (Dec. 1958)	35¢
T132. LINE SMASHER, Dick Friendlich	35¢